Bread and Tears

ALIBOR

Bread and Tears

Adèle Brook

VANTAGE PRESS
New York

FIRST EDITION

Published by Vantage Press, Inc.
516 West 34th Street, New York, New York 10001

Manufactured in the United States of America
ISBN: 0-533-10506-4

Library of Congress Catalog Card No.: 92-91072

0 9 8 7 6 5 4 3 2 1

To the vast number of women whose lives are interwoven with sacrifice and often heroism, but whose story no one was ever patient enough to listen to

Bread and Tears

1

Today is Sunday. Ruth was only four years old, but she knew. All the girls at the orphanage had clean uniforms with starched white collars. The convent's gloomy, long refectory, with tall windows and a gigantic crucifix on the front wall, looked prettier on Sunday. Fresh plants from the convent's greenhouse had been put there. Even the nuns' faces were more pleasant and friendly on Sunday.

At breakfast Ruth sat really straight in her chair and craned her neck to see her slice of bread, dripping with the honey she loved so much. The morning prayer seemed longer than usual, or was it because Ruth was so impatient and could hardly resist having a bite now? Only she knew that if she did she would be made to stand in a corner until it was time to join the "crocodile" to church. She was so craving something sweet. There was rice pudding or semolina at lunch sometimes, fruit or nuts, but that was not really sweet enough.

There was no honey for Ruth that Sunday. Tears welled up in her eyes and plopped down her face. She could not swallow the first mouthful of the dry bread. Thirstily she drank her milk; it was time to line up.

Unlike the other girls in the convent, little Ruth was not an orphan. After the Sunday morning mass, she would be permitted to visit her single mother until six o'clock in the evening, when Ruth had to return. Ruth's heart beat faster with excitement and fear. *Oh, what if Mummy does not come in time? She must be there. I shall run to her arms and feel her smooth cheeks,* she thought to herself.

The nuns had such sharp voices when they gave orders. When they sang in church their voices were much softer. Ruth's dark, sad eyes were wide open. It was the half-light in the church that made her so distressed. She sat still among the girls, the youngest of them all. She knew nothing about God yet. The whole time she looked at the statue of Saint Mary and Baby Jesus; she liked it. The statue reminded her of her own mother, whom she missed so much. "My mother is even more beautiful, and her name is Beatrix," Ruth whispered to herself. "Why did Sister Clotilda say she is a walking sin? What did Sister mean?"

The sound of last prayers reached the high vault of the church. The girls formed pairs in an orderly fashion and slowly, in silence, started to leave the church, sharply surveyed by the strict nuns. Ruth, led by a bigger girl, sighed impatiently.

Outside, in the light of the spring morning, Ruth saw her mother at once. She wanted to run, but her heart sank. Beatrix was not alone; a tall man was with her. Ruth had never seen him before. He and her mother both stepped forward to greet Mother Superior, who exchanged just a few words with them. Only then did the girl release Ruth.

Puzzled, Ruth walked towards her mother, kissed her, and looked shyly at the man, a question in her large eyes. He lifted her high above his head. When he put her down again, she did not laugh; she was astonished, as nobody had ever done this to her before. Then he bent down to her; now Ruth could see his dark hair brushed back and his kind, grey eyes, with a green glitter of fun in them. He talked to her gently. She didn't quite know what he was saying, but his calm, soft voice appealed to her immediately; still, she was not used to a man's voice, and she gave him another quizzical look.

Beatrix, gleaming with joy, asked, "Well, Carl, how do you like my little girl?" and she took Ruth's woollen hat off to show him her dark curls.

"Oh, what have they done to her?" Beatrix burst into tears. The child's hair was totally shaven off.

"I had lice; Karen and Elsa did, too," said Ruth in a thin little voice.

Carl quickly put the hat back on Ruth's devastated head and said tactfully, "It will soon grow back again. Ruth can keep her hat on; it is not that warm yet. Don't worry about it, Beatrix; your daughter is a darling as she is."

Carl was determined that nothing was going to spoil their Sunday. Prague can be a beautiful place in spring. Holding Ruth's hands, the bewildered child between them, the happy couple crossed the King Charles mediaeval bridge. There were parks on the range of hills above the river, where the cherry trees had just started to bloom. Carl took them up the hill by cable car, holding Ruth on his knees. It was new to her; she fidgeted and wanted down.

After a long walk, they stopped at a busy restaurant and had lunch there served outdoors. Ruth ate rather hungrily, and Carl wondered, "Are you sure you can eat a sweet after all that in your little tummy?"

"I only had plain bread this morning, no butter and honey."

Beatrix remembered. "I thought that you usually have honey on Sundays. The nuns keep their own bees, or don't they anymore?"

"Yes, Mummy, but I was being punished because I didn't kneel for the morning prayer. I was standing."

"But why didn't you, Ruth, if that is what you should have done?" asked Carl.

"I fell yesterday on the playground and hurt my knee."

"Then why didn't you say so?" Carl wondered.

"I did, but Sister Clotilda said that Jesus, our Lord, has suffered for me, so I can suffer for him."

Carl shook his head, and they all turned their attention to the cream cakes that the waiter was just serving. The waiter smiled at Ruth as her eyes followed his every move.

After that particular Sunday, Ruth's return to the orphanage was even harder than usual. That evening when Evangelina, the young novice in charge of the dormitory, noticed a wet pillow under Ruth's head, she understood and turned it over for her. She knew herself how it feels to cry oneself to sleep.

One month later Ruth woke up in a small room with lilac-coloured curtains on the window, wondering where the long dormitory with the white curtain drawn around Sister Angelica's bed at one end and Sister Mary's at the other was.

Carl came in with a smile, saying, "How is our princess this morning? Let's have a quick wash. It's all right; Mummy is here cooking breakfast. Now let's see what clothes are laid out here for you. Oh, this is the wrong side out . . . that's better. Now your shoes. Is this the left one?" Ruth's earnest face brightened and she giggled slightly.

"Off we go. I am so hungry." Carl laughed and rubbed his tummy.

Eating breakfast at her new home with Mummy and Carl was fun, like a game, and Ruth could have as much honey or jam as she liked.

"Now, young lady," Carl said, pulling a face that sent the girl into more giggles, unable to finish her milk, "I shall take you to a play group. You'll love it. There are lots of toys and games to play with, other girls as small as you are, and boys, too."

At the kindergarten, Carl introduced Ruth to her young teacher, gave Ruth a quick hug, and before leaving assured her, "Mummy will collect you after lunch."

When, some weeks later, it was Carl's turn to collect Ruth from the kindergarten, the teacher told him, "Your little girl must love you very much. I noticed she stressed to the children with pride, . . . 'I have a daddy, too; he was very far away.' "

"That is perhaps because I am a brand-new one." Carl smiled. Ruth had borne his surname since he married her mother. The teacher didn't know all the details.

Beatrix came back from her late shift at the hospital and asked, "How did you manage to get Ruth to bed? She usually looks for excuses to delay bedtime."

"I told her the story about the baby ant who was ill but was made well again with a speck of sugar."

Beatrix sat down and kicked the shoes off her tired feet. Carl sat next to her and put his arm around her shoulders. "I asked her, 'Do you want to say a prayer before I tuck you in?' 'Must I?' she asked. 'No,' I said. I don't like to force religion or politics on anybody. But then she jumped out, kneeled by her bed, and whispered, 'Thank you, God, for my mummy and daddy,' and jumped back into bed. I had to tuck her in again. Her hair has grown; she looks like a little boy now."

"You are marvellous, Carl. It shows what a good teacher you are; you have such patience with both of us."

"No problem. I love you, my pretty woman."

At the age of twenty-eight Carl Potocky was a truly educated man. He was very interested in classic literature, which he read in its original language. He played competitive chess even against the then-ruling champions. Also, he was a good athlete. He ran marathons, pole-vaulted, and was a fast swimmer and cyclist.

Carl came from a modest family that could afford the studies of the eldest of the three sons only by making great sacrifices. Carl was a keen student. He was given a chance for higher education, and thus he became an excellent teacher.

Carl's family had been disappointed in his choice of a wife and would not accept his marriage. The day Carl told his father, a tailor, that he was going to marry a young woman of twenty-three with an illegitimate child, his father threw his large scissors at him in anger. Carl never said a word about this or any other problems his marriage caused him, and did not expose Beatrix to his family's contempt.

A year passed. Nothing had changed when baby Lydia was born. Carl remained kind to Ruth and loved both children equally. He took his role as father very seriously and never indicated that Ruth was not his child. He treated Ruth as though she were his own, so Ruth, who had become extremely attached to him, believed he was her father.

Gently he introduced the institutionalized Ruth to a normal family life and soon managed to get rid of her deprivation syndrome. He led the schoolgirl through her growing up difficulties discreetly and with understanding, never reprimanding her for her shortcomings. He always gave her enough confidence by persuading her that she was clever enough and had many good qualities, as well as the ability to use them practically.

Each summer Carl was in charge of a children's holiday camp in the country. There, with all the other children, he taught Ruth games, things about nature, and how to swim. These were blissful days, and he loved to have his family close to him.

Carl did not mind spending evenings teaching Ruth maths, her weak spot, and encouraged her to greater efforts with jokes: "This way we would get rich easily, just by adding two more zeros to the multiplication, but we would end up in jail."

Carl surprised Beatrix when, one day, he made up his mind to go and visit her father, Emanuel, who was currently living in South Bohemia with his third wife, Agnes. Beatrix agreed reluctantly. She had not seen her father since he had let her down at the time she was expecting Ruth, but she did not want to show her anxiety.

"I'll show him his granddaughters, whether he likes it or not. A master printer, they say, is the aristocrat of the working class."

"You wait. If he takes you to his incredible private library, consider it a great honour."

As Ruth's happy years passed, Carl became more her confidant than Beatrix. He was always the first to be told everything. Another spring came when Ruth rushed home from school, burst in like an avalanche, and announced, "Great news, Daddy! I was chosen to represent our school at the president's birthday. I am to memorise a short poem and give him flowers. The boys' school is sending one of their pupils with me; each school in Prague sends a pair."

Carl smiled at Ruth's enthusiasm but was not given a chance to say how pleased and proud of her he was.

"Daddy, sit here and look important. I'll try it on you," she said.

"It is an honour to be the president's guinea pig," Carl remarked, taking the desired position in an armchair.

"Here I come. I bow. I present the posy. Here; you take it. The boy just stands beside me. Now I say my piece. I'll read it to you; tell me how it sounds before I memorize it."

Ruth had a good memory and could recite well quite naturally, so she had Carl's approval, which she sought each time she needed assurance.

Finally, the seventh of March 1925 came. Many delegations, diplomats, and members of the democratic government and the military arrived at Prague Castle, the residence of the first president, Prof. T. G. Masaryk.*

He was receiving them the whole morning. In the afternoon the second courtyard resounded with excited children's voices and no "shhh" of the nervous teachers could calm them down. There were more than a hundred delegates from Prague's primary schools.

The president's standard fluttered on the masthead; the atmosphere was festive and charged. When a serious man, wearing a morning coat, came and with a slow, dignified gesture indicated they might now go in, they grew silent all of a sudden and went forward in orderly pairs.

The exquisite Spanish Hall glittered with chandeliers of Bohemian crystal and huge mirrors on the walls. The children's eyes were shining in disbelief, some pressing a

---

*Prof. T. G. Masaryk (1850–1936) was the first president of the then-new Republic of Czechoslovakia following the signing of the Treaty of Versailles in 1918.

few spring blooms in their hands, some whispering to themselves the few words they were supposed to say.

The moment came for Ruth to step forward on the red carpet leading to a dais where, surrounded by serene men dressed in black and officers in uniforms, the seventy-five-year-old president sat.

Ruth, wearing her white First Communion dress and a white ribbon in her hair, stood before him, unusually shy. Then she saw a gentle smile on the old man's noble face, with his white beard and kind eyes behind a pince-nez, encouraging her. At this moment he ceased to be a well-known professor, great statesman, writer, and president. She recited her school's message perfectly, and he touched her dark curls to say he was pleased. She noticed the smile of one officer, who had the most medals and a black patch over his eye.*

Ruth came home delighted. "Daddy, it was in a beautiful hall, the president was so nice, he has a white beard and he stroked my hair, and, and . . . and—"

"Well," Carl said to calm her down, "he only listened to you; he was lucky not to see your handwriting." He kissed her and patiently listened to the rest of her experience.

In Ruth's school they had a young priest who once a week read from the Bible to them and explained each of the stories so that the children would understand them. On the day of Corpus Christi they took part in the procession. Ruth enjoyed it immensely, emptying her basket of petals on the way. Carl came to pick her up after the ceremony and said to the priest, "Your Bible lessons must be very persuasive. Ruth floated her doll in her mother's

---

*General Syrový

shopping basket on the waters of our bath, instead of the Nile, to see if it was possible that baby Moses survived."

The priest just smiled and patted Ruth's head.

2

Carl was an attentive husband and tolerant to extremes. He had always trusted his wife implicitly and never questioned her behaviour, so her frequent absences passed unnoticed, but her new clothes he did notice.

"Look, girls; isn't Mummy smart?" he remarked one Saturday evening.

Beatrix made gestures and movements like a fashion model to amuse them but felt uneasy, realising she should be more careful, considering her nurse's wages.

"I am going to the opera with my sister, Sidonie; what will you three do? Play chess again? Aren't you tired of teaching the girls, Carl?" Beatrix asked.

"No. I know it takes a great deal of time to learn. I don't mind."

"I must go now; don't wait up for me."

Lydia did her homework effortlessly. She did not need Carl's help and was always at the top of her class. She showed musical talent already and belonged to a children's choir. She had a steady temperament, compared with the nervous one Ruth had, so there were no problems there either.

Carl and Ruth went on with their game of chess when she remembered, "I forgot to tell Mummy I lost a button on my school jacket. Can you sew, Daddy?"

"I think so. My student years are not forgotten yet. But don't you think it is time for you to handle it? Better do it now; you can think about your next move while I look for a needle."

Carl searched in a drawer full of sewing materials and wool. Digging deeper, he touched a small box; wondering what it was, he opened it. Inside lay a ring, a large aquamarine encircled by small diamonds, quite clearly a genuine jewel. *That's strange,* he thought. *Beatrix never told me about it—why did she never show it to me?* he wondered.

Ruth called him back to the game but Carl couldn't take his mind off the ring. Why was Beatrix hiding it? Who else would give her such an expensive jewel but Edward Schwarz, Ruth's natural father? Carl tormented himself, *Beatrix told me the whole unhappy story, about the fact that Edward was reported missing in 1916 when Ruth was born and how she was let down by his Jewish family and her own Catholic one as well. She was nineteen, a student nurse, and had to leave Ruth in her first year with a retired nurse and later had no choice but to put Ruth in a convent orphanage so she would be able to work.*

Her past was not important to me, I accepted it and forgot about it. I loved her, he argued with himself.

"Here is your jacket, Ruth. Put it where it belongs and fold up the chess game. It is time to prepare for bed, both of you." Carl had to force himself to speak calmly.

"Mummy is tired; she hardly speaks to me lately," Ruth complained.

Carl was astonished how Ruth also, in direct contrast to Lydia, sensed the tense atmosphere. "Yes, we must try to help her more with the housework," he suggested.

The girls safely in bed, Carl asked a neighbour to look in on them whilst he went to bring his wife home from the opera. There he waited in the dark, watching the exit. He could see her now with a well-dressed man in his late thirties. They walked in the direction of the tram stop, where they parted as the tram came. Carl was unable to move—he recognised Edward from an old photograph. He had to act and come to his senses quickly. He jumped in the tram behind a group of people.

"Oh, it's you." Beatrix looked surprised but composed.

"I came to take you home." Carl's voice, not easy to control, was low. His wife was silent, her eyes half-closed, looking tired.

Carl's mind was restless. *I must pull myself together! I must wait to see if she herself explains to me what is going on. I don't want to reproach her for anything. Oh God, I don't want to lose her; what am I to do?* he reflected ruefully.

At home Beatrix went straight to the bedroom and began getting ready for bed. That gave Carl time to think about how his new job might solve it all.

Next morning they both behaved like normal and Carl said cheerfully, "Well, girls, Sunday is a good day. Now I have you all here, I'll give you some good news. I have been offered a position as headmaster of a boys' school in a beautiful place near the Spa Marienbad."

Beatrix remained silent.

Ruth jumped up, saying, "Does that mean no school for us?"

"You would like that, wouldn't you? Don't worry; we'll find a nice girls' school for you two until the government decides for co-education—soon, I hope. What about you, Beatrix? How would you like it? We could manage there on my salary, so you would have more free time on your hands."

"We can discuss it later. I . . . er . . . um, I don't really know; when must you decide?" She hesitated.

"In about two months' time or so," answered Carl with pain in his voice.

Several long weeks passed. Carl waited patiently until the crucial evening when Beatrix wanted to talk things over with him.

"You are so good at explaining everything to the girls, especially to Ruth, I want you to tell her that she is not your daughter," Beatrix began.

"But whatever for? We agreed long ago, when she was small and I gave her my name, not to complicate her life. I am her father. I act like one, and I love her. It would destroy her trust in me. You don't want that. Why now? What is the matter with you?"

"I have to tell you that Edward came back from the Russian POW camp a long time ago. He looked for me in vain and gave up. Now he has found me, we have been seeing each other and realised, after several meetings, that we still love each other. I know how unfair and cruel it is to you, but I intend to go back to him eventually."

"I am shattered myself and can hardly believe it. How do you want me to say all this to the poor child? I wouldn't know how. She is so trusting; how can I hurt her like this?"

"What do you mean, hurt her? Edward *is* her father!"

"So let *him* tell her. I refuse to give her such upsetting news; she is a sensitive teenager." Carl held his face in his hands. "Edward knows nothing about her. I watched her grow up, nursed her, comforted her in your absence. I know her needs, her faults, her virtues, her tastes, and her anxieties. What does he know about his own daughter?"

"You are prejudiced; he will learn to know her. But she will certainly take the news better from you; just think about it. In the meantime you can accept your new post out of Prague and leave the rest of it to the solicitors."

Carl was appalled. He attacked Beatrix abusively: "Just like that! Have you no feelings at all? You expect me to give up Lydia as well? You are ruining my life and want me to accept it with joy? The thought is killing me. Even if I break it to the girls gently and eloquently, they will be flabbergasted."

It was difficult to hide his sorrow from the observant Ruth. Carl had to face the sad facts reasonably, be as composed as possible, and admit that this inexorable truth had to come from him. Still, Carl put up a tremendous fight, made scenes, and even started to drink. He was out of his mind, but it was all in vain. There was no way he could prevent this disaster. Still he postponed it, hoping against hope that there would be some better solution.

Late one night Ruth woke up. She could hear her parents' discussion again, only this time the door of their bedroom was ajar. She could hear every word.

"Beatrix, please, for the sake of the girls, do not split up our family."

Barefoot, Ruth approached the door. Carl, his defiance now subdued, had done his utmost to persuade Beatrix and now, dispirited, pleaded with her once more. Ruth could see him by her mother's chair, on his knees, pitiful in his agony.

"Don't leave me!" Carl's voice rose, then ended in a whisper.

Ruth became distraught; her insecurity and the old feelings of deprivation were back. She could not cope with her parents' crisis. Her adolescent girl's mind overreacted: *I want to die!* The fear of losing her father, to whom she still clung helplessly, was overwhelming. *I am in their way. Oh, I want to die!*

Ruth managed to creep into the bathroom. There she remembered the half-full bottle of sleeping tablets and took them all. Soon Ruth became drowsy and was just beginning to think gratefully it would soon be over when, as if through a thick cloud, she heard her mother scream. Then Ruth lost consciousness; she woke up in hospital after they had pumped her stomach out.

Reason prevailed and Carl gave up. Divorce proceedings started, and it was obviously going to be a lengthy, painful affair for him. He suggested it would be wise to say nothing to the confused Ruth but send her away from the harmful atmosphere at home to a boarding school.

* * *

At the age of fourteen Ruth was sent to a German commercial college in North Bohemia. There, unaware of the changes at home, and in new surroundings, she slowly calmed down, happier among students her own age.

Carl got the first report that indicated Ruth liked the school:

> As you know, Daddy, I am talkative as a parrot, so my German is improving. My Gabelsberger shorthand is all right if they don't rush me, but with the bookkeeping I miss your help; the ciphers haunt me at night. It is not my favourite subject, I don't think I shall ever be an accountant.
>
> There is no opportunity for swimming, so I started to play tennis, but I am a lousy player. Only my new friends Greta and Hilde are patient enough to play with me. There will be plenty of ski activities in winter and we shall have dancing lessons as well. I have befriended several more girls, and one is helping me with my dress. There is needlework on the curriculum, which will also be in the second year. . . .

These letters were not frequent but were encouraging. They sounded happier each time. Beatrix, forced by remorse, visited Ruth there just once. For the holidays she sent Ruth and her sister, Lydia, to stay with Aunt Sidonie in Moravia. Oddly enough, Aunt Sidonie had more understanding for Ruth than her mother, who was too busy sorting out her own personal life.

The second school year in the German-speaking Sudetenland ended, and Ruth joined the YWCA to spend a holiday at the French resort Arcachon, with the French section. This was a pleasant stay on the Atlantic coast with a great deal of freedom, games, and swimming, with girls of several different nationalities, ending with a tour of Paris. Ruth enjoyed this summer and scarcely had time to send home a postcard.

Ruth's parents were endlessly attempting to resolve their marriage/divorce problems and thought it better to have her out of the way, which meant going from one boarding school to another.

3

Still far too young for finishing school, Ruth nevertheless was sent to one in Switzerland. The grief of being away from home for so long became hard to bear. It was not only because she came on a dull September day, when Lake Geneva was grey, the sky was grey, and so were her thoughts. She wrote to Carl:

Dear Daddy,

I arrived at Morges all right, just tired after the 24 hours long journey by train. The headmistress, Madame Vialone, met me at the small station, where the express does not stop. I had to change at Lausanne. The panorama of the Alps was hidden in the clouds; not even the many gulls and a few swans could make this place by the lake look more cheerful.

At the school I was accommodated in a small, pleasant room with a view of the lake. Madame Vialone presented me to the governesses and some two dozen girls. I had my first evening meal with them, wondering why they were giggling all the time.

The next morning the sky was blue; the Alps were silhouetted in the distance, behind a sapphire blue lake. It was simply breathtaking. You like mountains; I wish you could see it.

This is a strict school in every way. Madame Vialone is adamant about punctuality for staff and pupils alike. None of the girls is allowed out of the school unescorted. A girl from Morocco, Augusta, is a practising Catholic and goes to the nearby church every day, but with a governess. Solange shares a room with her and gossips about her. Apparently, Augusta kneels by her bed every night to pray, her beautiful long hair down her back, looking angelic, but in fact she is a nasty, squalling, rancorous hypocrite of a creature. I am always left out of the older girls' "secret" conversations. They stop their whispering when I approach as if I were a baby—what do they think I am? A sycophant? . . .

One girl is friendly and charming. Her name is Camille. She is so considerate and speaks to me slowly. She understands that I am still not accustomed to the French language; it takes time . . .

I miss you, Daddy.

Ruth

Here she was, a timid, withdrawn, homesick teenager who had a hard time at the beginning, as her French was not up to the required standard. Gradually it became less difficult, yet her letters to Carl were now rare and short, unconsciously letting him know her feelings of frustration and lack of friendliness in this institution.

For some time now separate letters had come from her mother and from Carl, so Ruth understood that she had to write separate answers to different addresses. By the time Christmas approached, Ruth had gradually managed fluent conversational French, mostly thanks to Camille, who was not too proud, in spite of being frequently given as an example to the rest of the pupils, to spend time with Ruth.

Everybody went home for the Christmas holidays except Ruth. Instead Carl was coming to take her on a skiing holiday to Zermatt, one of the most popular ski resorts below the Matterhorn, so she looked forward to it. A letter and a gift from her mother arrived at the school for her, but her mother's absence was still painful—there was no way she could make it up to Ruth.

Carl tried so hard to give her a good time and make her happy, Ruth felt sorry for him, and to please him she tried to be happy. She was delighted to be with him, yet it was all tinged with sadness, which both tried to forget.

"I can't keep up with you, tiresome daredevil," he joked. "That's enough skiing for this morning; what do you think I am, a world champion? Let's go down to the village, have some of those goodies they serve there, and I'll buy you a bell they use here to hang around the calves' necks so that they don't get lost."

They took several pictures of each other in the snow and asked a skier to take a snapshot of them both to finish the film—it was now ready at the photo shop. Ruth had a good laugh looking at the photo.

"You look funny, Daddy. It's worth a frame."

Ruth bought one with the local "decor" for Carl to remember this holiday, little suspecting this would be the last time he acted as her daddy to her.

On the funicular up to Gornograd they admired the mountaintops in the distance, Carl holding her around the shoulders. Then he asked how far she had advanced in French literature and what else she was learning.

"Well, you'll be happy to hear that I know how to eat a banana with a knife and fork. In the housekeeping classes I cooked fondue, which curdled, and we were instructed how to put the right drinks into the right glasses. I also can recite several *Fables de La Fontaine, par exemple,* the cautious one, *'La Cigale et la Fourmie.'* Satisfied?"

Carl pretended to fall off the bench with laughter.

In spite of all the luxuriant days they had together, Ruth sensed there was something wrong. Carl knew that tomorrow would be the last day of this togetherness and, after that, their lives would never be the same again. Tomorrow he must tell her the facts about her background, of which she knew nothing so far. Actually, that was why he had come to see her—oh, what a task!

"It is a sunny day; we'll get a tan. I wish Mummy were with us, too, but I expect she would have brought Lydia with her as well and that would have been too expensive."

Ruth turned to Carl, waiting for his explanation, and saw a worried, earnest expression on his face; she looked back at him again, frightened, realising he was preparing to tell her something, some bad news. Carl hated to bring bad news to people; this was how he always hesitated when faced with such a situation. Her heart thudded with suppressed fear of another blow.

"Let's sit here on the deck chairs; it is peaceful and warm on the balcony. All the skiers have gone to the slopes. Mummy has her reasons, much more serious than the question of money. You'll see what I mean. Listen to me and please don't interrupt me; it would make my task harder than it already is."

Carl started to speak slowly, in a low voice, as if every word caused pain to his throat.

"When I met your mother at the house of your godmother, Flora, where I tutored her children, you were three years old. So, you see, I was not your father. Due to the war and other circumstances, your father was unable to marry your mother. You haven't forgotten the orphanage, I know! You wouldn't have been there in the first place if I was your father. Because your Grandpa Emanuel did not help her, Mummy had to put you there and go to work, at least until it was possible for her to look after you herself."

Ruth looked at the beautiful mountainous scenery

and the skiers below. The view of the sunlit Matterhorn became blurred as her eyes started to fill with tears.

"That became possible when I fell in love with your mother and offered to marry her, not knowing that your real father, who had been reported missing, presumed dead, did come back from a POW camp in Russia the same year."

Carl spoke slower and slower but did not stop. "Your mother and I are now divorced. At first I wanted to fight a legal battle for both of you girls. But now your natural father is taking over, I would certainly lose you and only separate you two girls. Your mother would resent it, and I don't want her to hate me.

"The time has come for us to part. I accepted a position at the boys' school in Marienbad—that is where I live now—and you, in the future, are going to live with your father, Edward, after he marries Beatrix."

Ruth was silent for a long time. They both looked at the mountaintops silhouetted in the distance; then she flung her arms round Carl's neck, tears running down her cheeks. He was her lodestar, her fixation.

"I want to go with you," Ruth whispered.

Carl was so moved he could not go on. He just held her until her cries had quietened and her body stopped shaking.

"There is still a great deal you must be told to understand. I love your mother dearly; therefore, I must let her go. All I want is for her to be happy. I don't know your father, Edward Schwarz, personally, but if your mother loves him so much as to leave me, then he must be a good man. He remained single; that proves he never loved anybody else but her.

"Since I have learned of the plan as it is, I have tried to find out enough about your father, Edward, to be able to tell you about him. He comes from an assimilated Jewish family, is certainly a respectable and successful businessman, is well off, and has a comfortable flat in Prague and a country house, where his old mother lives. So, you see, you shall have a grandma. Unfortunately, she has been in a wheelchair for many years. Mixed marriages are not such a crime as they used to be in the old days—everything will be all right; you'll see."

"I don't want to meet those strange people; if you must live elsewhere, Daddy, take me with you. I have your name, so I am your daughter," Ruth now interjected.

"Be reasonable, Ruth." Carl tried to comfort her as she was again sobbing in his arms. "Of course you shall always be my precious daughter; I always loved you, ever since I saw you so pathetic with your hair shaved off. Then and there I decided never to let anybody hurt you again. We'll keep in touch as we do now, even if sometimes I cannot read your handwriting. I want to know how you are getting on. Promise me you will go on with your studies. You certainly have been given the chance, but you must work."

"Don't you want to have me with you after I finish school? When everything with Mummy is settled, we can live together. Doesn't Lydia want that, too?"

Carl could hardly calm her down. He hugged her tight.

"You know I would do that if it were possible, but legally I have no right to take you with me. Lydia takes things very practically for her age. She wants to stay with Mummy, so I am going to let Beatrix have custody. In fact, Lydia loves herself enough, she does not need anybody's love, and she does not need me for maths either; she is top of her class, no problem there."

Holding each other, they looked across the beautiful valley covered with snow, glittering in the sun; against the background of blue sky, the great Matterhorn was towering above the rest of the white and blue mountains. Ruth looked at all this beauty through her tears, feeling sorry for them both.

Carl realised that while he wanted to let Beatrix have all the happiness she sought, he had to deny it to this tearful, thin little creature who so desperately wanted his protection, as she always had in the past.

The next morning they travelled together back to the school in Morges. Before the heartbreaking good-bye, Ruth asked Carl not to mention to Madame Vialone anything about the new situation.

"She gets her monthly payment; that is all she wants anyhow," Ruth said.

It started to rain. Ruth stood by her window watching Carl get into a taxi down below on the wet pavement. Her eyes followed the departing car, through the drops of rain dripping down the glass, until it was out of sight. The lake was not shimmering; it was grey today. She threw herself on her bed, sobbing uncontrollably, until her friend Camille knocked on the door.

"May I come in? Are you ready for dinner? You look *épouvantable*; go and wash your face and change your creased blouse. Put away that soaked handkerchief. I saw your father leave—that's no reason to look like a *chat noyé*. Let me see . . . that's better. Now tidy up your hair; hurry up or we'll both be late." Camille was sympathetic, but also sensible. She kissed Ruth's cheek; they at last went into the *salle à manger*.

4

Nothing important happened. Everything ticked precisely, as the Swiss clocks and watches do. With the full daily schedule at school, time passed quickly, and soon came the school summer holiday. Everybody went home except Ruth. A letter came from Carl explaining gently and thoughtfully to her: " . . . don't be sad, dear girl; you'll have an interesting holiday. Madame Vialone has arranged for you to stay at a farm below the Jura Mountains, which I think will suit you fine, as you like the outdoors. . . . I am sorry," etc., etc.

Ruth cried secretly and bitterly into her pillow, which she had not done since her last days at the orphanage. She was desperately homesick. Bravely, she didn't show a sign of disappointment to the others, not even to Camille, her reasonable and understanding friend, who was always kind to her.

Accompanied by one of the governesses, Ruth travelled to a mountain village. They took a slow, slow little train at Morges. Its steam engine was puffing up to the foothills of the Jura on its wooden tracks rather noisily. The scenery was tranquil—fields, woods, vineyards, farms, meadows, and many cows. The little train went on puffing heavily, to pass more meadows, pastures, and cows.

"Have the Swiss a cow as their emblem, as England

has a lion, France the cock, and Russia a bear?" Ruth asked the smiling governess.

"No, the Swiss symbol is the edelweiss," was her answer.

At the farm Ruth felt at home in one single day. The old farmer was jolly and teased her constantly, calling her *"ma belle."* She soon learned to call him "Tall William" as all the villagers did. His sweet-natured, quiet wife was nice, too. She must have been a pretty woman once. Now she had white hair and gentle blue eyes, and her name was Hortense. She was like a quiet white mouse, silent, calm, always busy in her kitchen. Every day she wore a clean white apron over her dark, long skirt. Ruth did small errands and daily chores for her quite eagerly; she wanted to be useful. She even learned how to tend the hay.

In his younger days Tall William had been a dragoon in the Swiss army. One morning before Ruth got up, he found his old military blanket, saddle, and bridle. Soon, there stood his mare, ready for Ruth to ride. The farmer explained to Ruth the basic rules of how to handle a horse and instructed her to press her knees firmly against the horse and sit up straight.

"Off you go, and don't sit like a lump; move with the horse."

Ruth was also allowed to drive the mare in a rake to harvest the hay.

Teaching Ruth to ride was not the only pleasant surprise Tall William had for her. Sometimes he took her up to the Jura Mountains for a day. They would sit in silence, admiring the view for hours with utmost reverence. Ruth never dared to disturb his meditation; she respected the simple old man very much. She waited until he seized the basket, saying, "Well, I got hungry. The exercise in the fresh air gave me an appetite; how about you?"

Ruth nodded.

"Let us see what Hortense has prepared for us."

Whatever it was, at more than a thousand metres above sea level it tasted heavenly.

"All this is God's creation; it stops a man from being too arrogant, *ma chère,*" said Tall William as he went on cutting a slice of Gruyère.

Tall William was the model of a man in Ruth's eyes at this time, when Ruth was a child, and that was how she would think of him always. In the evenings they used to sit in the large, old farm kitchen. There was a huge chimney with bacon, hams, and salami hanging there as well as garlands of onions and garlic. There was a wireless at the house, but it was not switched on very often. While Hortense did her knitting, they would listen to Tall William's stories; sometimes visitors would come and would be invited into his wine cellar for a glass or two of his own best wine.

Most days Ruth and Tall William picked fruit in his orchard, walked through his vineyards to see if there were any pests, and with horse and carriage took lunch to the people working Tall William's fields and vegetable plantations. There were no cars in the village at the time, with the exception of the local doctor's, and only the mayor and Tall William had a tractor each, as they had the largest farms.

On some rainy days Ruth, Hortense, and Tall William were busy cracking last year's walnuts—sacks of them which were then sent to be prepared for cooking oil. On mild evenings, the three of them used to sit on a wooden bench in the front garden; from there they could see the lights of Évian shining across Lac Léman.

Ruth learned to love Tall William's woods, where there was a small lake in which she used to swim. On Sundays they all went to the Protestant church on the village green, where they sang together with the local choir, trained by the vicar. Tall William had a strong baritone voice; Ruth's he called "*bébé* soprano."

On Sunday afternoons Ruth went with other young people for a walk up the hills; "Le Pasteur" was happy to take groups of them with him. He knew a great deal about natural history, botany in particular, and his lessons in the sweet mountain air, under the beautiful firs and pines, were much more interesting than those in the classroom.

To her great regret Ruth could not stay for "Les Vendanges," when, Tall William told her, there would be festivities and outdoor dances. However she was able to enjoy the Swiss National Festival, always held on August first *, with the mayor's speech, fireworks, and bonfires; she joined all the other girls from the village, also wearing the traditional costume of "Canton de Vaud," which dear Hortense had lent her for the occasion.

Most unwillingly, mainly because her friend Camille had finished her term and would not be there anymore, Ruth went back to school. Tall William said, "You must be educated into a grand lady, not grow wild as the red poppy in the field. I cannot promise to write; my hand is much too heavy for writing. We shall miss your company, Hortense and I. Au revoir, ma belle."

When the second year of school was over, Ruth stopped asking to come home and went for her vacation to

---

*Date of the sermon at Mont Rutli and the uprising of the Cantons against the Hapsburgs in A.D. 1491.

the farm below the Jura Mountains without the slightest objection.

Tall William waited for her at the small, picturesque station with his horse and carriage. Ruth leapt out of the train, ran to the tall, old farmer, and kissed him, hanging onto his neck with her legs in the air, her suitcase still on the platform. She was so hungry for love after the long term at a school with such a strict atmosphere and all the austerity, and she was happy to know she would find plenty of love here. And so she spent another two months of wonderful holiday with the dear old people.

In the centre of the village there was a fountain of clear, cold water where Ruth used to rinse their washing just as other girls did, usually on Mondays. They would chat there, making a noise like a flock of geese. She made many young friends in the village, and her French improved more there than in school.

To her great regret, Ruth was told that after this holiday she would be sent to another boarding school, this time in England. There was no way of knowing if or when she would be able to come to her paradise below the Jura Mountains again. They were parting with tears. Tall William tried to joke, saying, "You are growing into a pretty young woman. That future husband of yours, wherever he is now, will be a lucky man."

Ruth promised to come back with the "lucky man" and some children, maybe. Hortense just hugged Ruth without a word. It was so touching. Ruth turned away quickly and climbed onto the carriage. Tall William put her suitcase next to her and was ready to take her back again to the railway station. On the train her sad eyes followed the scenery she now knew. She wanted to memorise it, not knowing what the future held for her.

5

Another boring boarding school, again another governess waiting, this time by the boat train at Victoria Station in London; oh, schools are all the same! Ruth sighed, stepping off the train straight into the open arms of smiling Camille.

"Mais quelle surprise, que c'est que tu fais ici?" Ruth said.

"Stop right there; you are not permitted to speak French or even Chinese at our establishment. I heard you were coming, I said I knew you, so they sent me to pick you up and take you to Kingston on Thames. You are a rarity; they have never had a pupil from your country."

"Don't tell me you are here without a governess."

"Yes. As I am twenty and you nearly nineteen, we are treated as senior students here, all free after classes. Let's go; the driver is waiting in the minibus, which usually takes us on our excursions, to sports, theatres, concerts, museums, and exhibitions. All is culture here, my dear, emphasis on English language and literature, of course, but no drill as in Morges. Get in; I'll tell you all about it on the way."

"I have never heard you speak so much before, Mademoiselle de Roche*; you sound so happy."

*Camille had a French name because she was descended from French Protestant aristocrats, the Huguenots, who had lived in Switzerland since the French Revolution.

"I think you'll like it here, too. The private school for ladies is run by three spinster sisters, nicknamed 'the Brontës,' but you will address them all as 'Miss Williams.' The eldest is kind of a matron; she runs the household. The food is quite decent. The middle one teaches English, very fussy about pronunciation; the youngest is all etiquette, aesthetics, literature, and art."

"It sounds fine to me," said Ruth when she had a chance.

"Oh, yes. The single rooms are small but comfortable; mine is next to yours. Some rooms are shared by two or three girls, all from different countries. Two are Swedish, but they put Ganvar with Miriam, a Hungarian girl. Ingrid has the best room in the house; she is apparently a daughter of a steel magnate. Ganvar is more fun—a very beautiful blonde—you wait till you see her swim; she stays underwater like a dolphin, incredible. Then there is a serious Danish girl. On the second floor there are three 'Brunhildas' from different parts of Germany, one from Austria, two 'frogs,' two English girls, two Scottish lassies, and the two of us make it fifteen in all. It is a problem in keeping the nationalities apart. There is a penny fine for each non-English word spoken. Oh yes, two more snags. We have to change for dinner, very old-fashioned that, and on Sunday morning we have to go to our respective churches. You'll come with me to a Protestant one, won't you?"

"Yes, Camille, anything you say. I suppose it should be the synagogue now; actually, I was baptized in a Catholic church. Only you can persuade the most determined pagan to go to church, you stubborn Calvinist."

"Here we are, just in time for tea, then I'll give you a guided tour."

Far more relaxed, Ruth's letters to Carl now reflected her self- confidence. She wrote:

. . . I shall be so ladylike you'll hate me. I can recite "All the world's a stage . . . " by heart; also, some of us joined the local theatrical company to play small parts in *Hiawatha* (Longfellow)—my looks and speech are quite authentic; I make a fine squaw.

I have been invited to go home for Xmas with Camille de Roche to Geneva; it is my favourite town. We shall go up the mountain Salève to see the *imposant* Mont Blanc ruling in the Alps, then ski down to France, where her elder brother, an architect, has a chalet; we can stay there if we promise to cook for him, poor Claude! It is in Chamonix, where I will think of you. I keep our photo from Zermatt on my dressing table and take it with me wherever I travel, even when it is just for a few days.

I asked Mummy about the Xmas holidays, and she has no objections. I don't think Lydia will miss me as long as I send her a Xmas present, which I will do, of course. My present from home was early, as I needed a set of lingerie and a new outfit for England, new things for tennis (the school has a grass court), and we do ride once a week, so I had to be fitted for that as well as for the swimming pool. Thanks to you, I can compete with Ganvar in swimming.

I left Madame Vialone with no regret. Since Camille and the other girls I knew had left, there were all newcomers.

All my childish clothes, mostly too small for me, were given to the Red Cross. I am afraid I spend a great deal of those large white bank notes here. The piano lessons are not included in the fee. I don't think I am any good at it, but I would be the only one not taking any. Ingrid, the Swedish girl, could give concerts already. But as you used to tell me, one can't know everything, but one can try. My pigtail has been cut off, but I am not too grown up yet not to say I love you; Daddy, please love me, too.

Ruth

The time was flying. The classes became more serious, and Ruth had to work harder to keep up with the other pupils, including "Minerva," as Camille was nicknamed.

In January, George V passed away and everybody from the boarding school, teachers included, went to London for the funeral. They saw the unfortunate new king, Edward VIII, so sad, walking alone in the procession and all of Europe's kings, princes, and presidents, representing their respective countries in the cortège.

Subsequently the crisis of Edward VIII and Mrs. Simpson erupted and filled the newspapers with large headlines. It was the year of three kings.

In the spring, Ruth wrote enthusiastically to Carl again:

Dear Dad,

This school is so fabulous, there is never a dull moment. I don't keep a diary as some girls do. I prefer to tell everything to you. Maybe you keep my letters; oh, what a collection! I keep yours under my pillow—my friends think they are from a boyfriend.

The school's minibus took us, the young ladies, to Stratford-upon-Avon for the day with baskets full of goodies. We had a picnic on the way in a wood. Do not imagine the Bohemian virgin wood, just a woodland. We visited the famous town and went to the performance of *The Taming of the Shrew*—to show us how Shakespeare should be spoken.

Last Saturday, Camille, Ganvar, and I had permission to go to London on our own. We had tea at Lyons Cornerhouse and then saw a great performance of *The Barber of*

Seville in the Covent Garden Opera House—that is, without Ganvar. She said she'd skip the opera and went to some party. We all had to meet at the station to come back together. Ganvar, of course, nearly missed the train. She is always late; that's normal for her. The other day she sauntered somewhere and had to get in by pushing up the window of our study. . . .

Another letter followed in June 1936:

Dear Dad,

We went for an interesting outing to Southampton to watch the maiden voyage of the ship *Queen Mary* on May 27. It was an unforgettable sight. Surrounded by dozens of small boats as satellites, she was tugged by two pilot vessels out of the harbour. After the pilots left her, tall, proud, and majestic, she sailed to New York. We were all enthralled by the way the gigantic ship moved with grace and dignity. I wrote about this to Mummy as well.

By this time, Ruth felt quite at home in England, but her studies abroad were ending and she had to return to Prague. She wrote to Carl:

. . . You know how much I was longing to go home, but now, when the time has come and my stay here is soon ending, I don't look forward to leaving. It is not that I am frightened of the examination at the Prague University so much as of the fact that I shall have to face my "new family," so to speak. I'll miss your backing and advice. Please, tell me in your next letter what I should do, how I am supposed to behave, what is expected of me. I have become a stranger to my own family, let alone to another one.

Love,
Ruth

6

The international express train slowed down and drove into the main station at Prague. Ruth's heart missed a beat. She approached the window, shy and indecisive. Mummy and Edward met her as she stepped down. Embarrassed by Edward's embrace and Mummy's amusement over Ruth's embarrassment, she blushed. They were surprised by her elegant and grown-up appearance. Edward called a porter and with laughter counted her suitcases.

Ruth quickly remembered Carl's advice: "Just be yourself, tactful, polite, and ladylike. You have been trained for it!"

Lydia was now a pretty girl of fifteen, and as Ruth was unpacking she came to negotiate with her big sister, to swap something for her swimsuit. Lydia loved Ruth's real silk stockings and heavenly blouse; she was sorry to have much smaller shoes to swap.

She was now so good at the piano that Ruth did not dare touch it, and Ruth's singing could not compete with Lydia's perfect soprano. Lydia was preparing to start at the teaching college the following September.

Beatrix and Ruth were both invited for a weekend to the country house; Grandma Emily wished to meet Ruth. Edward was showing off his attractive, well-dressed wife-to-be, and she was all smiles and seemed not to give Carl a second thought; Ruth could not bear it. In return she was indifferent towards Edward. He certainly found it difficult to approach her; he gave her a golden bracelet with pretty charms as a homecoming gift. She turned it on her wrist to look at each one of them.

"Well, Ruth, do you like it?" Edward asked rather awkwardly.

"It is lovely. Thank you, sir," Ruth murmured with her eyes cast down.

Beatrix reprimanded Ruth impatiently, "Edward is your father; you needn't call him 'sir.' "

But Ruth lowered her head even more and gave no answer.

On the other hand, Ruth liked the old lady; she had the same sad, dark eyes as Ruth and was very sympathetic to her.

"Give the girl a chance to know us. She is shy. No wonder; all these changes are hard for her," Grandma defended Ruth, then called the maid. "Jeanine, bring some of the homemade ice cream for the ladies and lots of whipped cream, please."

It looked gorgeous.

"Ah, a smile after all. Enjoy it now. When you have finished I want you to push my wheelchair in the garden; we'll have a woman-to-woman talk."

Ruth took Grandma Emily around the lovely garden.

"I like it here, Grandma—it is so peaceful. There are so many roses; I am also fond of roses," Ruth said.

"You know, my dear, that you can stay with me whenever you wish, don't you?"

"Yes, Grandma, I would like that."

"You don't seem to be very happy. These are the consequences of your late grandpa's destructive interference in Edward's life. Morice had a stubborn nature and was absolutely uncompromising. I had no say in this, nor in any other matters, ever. Yet it could have been all so simple just to accept you and your mother. He ruined my life and now even yours."

Grandma Emily paused for a moment, going back in her memories as far as her young days.

"After my father had the first heart attack, he asked his young, efficient director to look after the factory for me, if anything should happen to him. Morice, your grandpa, did as he had promised, and when my father died I was passed to him together with the factory, so to speak.

"Morice married me when I was seventeen; he was fifteen years my senior. He never loved me and didn't expect any love from me. I was to respect him and obey."

Grandma stopped for a moment; her eyes were so sad when she went on remembering the despotic man who had terrorised his family and staff. "He also died of a heart attack, in 1918, before his three sons came back from World War I. Do I bore you, my dear?"

"No, Grandma, I am listening. You must have been bewildered by all those unhappy events."

"There are no more relatives for you to meet. Your Uncle Oscar is dead; he was a doctor, had a Russian wife, and left behind him a boy, Victor. Your Uncle Richard and his wife, Rachel, went to live in Chile, I think. I suffered a stroke at the age of forty-five, and after that I was unable to help anybody. I ended up in this wheelchair, and since then I have had Jeanine to protect and care for me. No matter what my husband Morice did, she would not run away as the other girls did; she would not flinch or blink when he screamed something rude at her or even hinted bodily harm. She would wheel me away, her chin up, as if she had not heard a thing.

"So, you see, I have had a well-sheltered life, but an empty one. I have often thought about you—where you live, how you actually look, a little like I used to at your age. I must ask Jeanine to find some old pictures to show you.

"You are bright as well. I hear a good education for a girl is more important these days than it was at the beginning of the century. I am glad you are getting the best; it will give you more independence. Now, my dear, push me back to the house, please. Call the old girl of mine; I must rest."

"Yes, Grandma. Don't worry about me; I'll be all right. It's just that Carl . . . " Ruth could not go on; the words stuck in her throat.

"I understand how you feel about all these changes. Remember I want to be your friend."

"You already are, Grandma." Ruth kissed her cheek and that was settled.

Ruth made many more visits to Grandma Emily; they used to speak French together. It was astonishing that the old lady still remembered what she had learned in school and from her governess so long ago. Whenever they met, Ruth wanted her to smile; she would twirl around for her to show off her new dress and tell her funny stories about school or a performance she had seen lately, especially ballet.

Grandma Emily Schwarz met Ruth's future husband briefly, but she died shortly before Ruth's wedding, in 1941.

* * *

Ruth's life in Prague was filled with studies until she finished all her exams successfully; she even achieved a first in English language and literature and she did well in French, where the weak marks for grammar had been well compensated by the high ones for her fluent conversation and accurate accent.

She had good reason to be a little proud of herself and sent photocopies of her diplomas to Carl. He was now headmaster at the boys' school in Marienbad. A fat woman looked after him. His letters were rather guarded in tone but showed that he was pleased with Ruth's progress. Ruth understood that not wanting to cause any trouble by his influence, he was tactfully withdrawing into the background now that she was getting used to her "new family" and he thought she did not need his help anymore.

Ruth had already applied for a vacancy with Air France and was waiting to be called for an interview, and there were still days when she longed for Carl's loving guidance and reassurance, feeling vulnerable without it. When the interview came, to pluck up her courage Ruth tried to remember what advice Carl would have given her—"act positively"—and she did.

Calm and composed, Ruth entered the large, elegant office of the director of Air France's branch in Prague, wearing a purple tailor-made suit with the jacket trimmed with black fur and matching hat. As she approached the desk his eyes went from her tapering long legs upwards. He asked her to sit down and politely offered her a cigarette, which she equally politely declined. He spoke French to her and scrutinised her diplomas. Constantly examining her appearance, he explained to her that the airline would open for business in about six months. Only after all the staff were chosen would the training begin, some of it in London, the first part in the Prague offices, and she would be notified in time.

That was it! Ruth could not believe it and was overjoyed. She landed herself a job as one of the first air hostesses in Europe!

7

Then came Ruth's first winter back home. Edward took "his three girls" for a short skiing holiday to the Tatra Mountains in Slovakia, as he felt they all needed a break.

While Lydia was already up the ski-lift with a group, Ruth was still limping to it, as she had just hurt her knee. A skier approached her, saying, "Did you have a fall? Is it your knee? Sit over there. I am a doctor; let's have a look at it."

"No, thanks, that won't be necessary; it is not serious." Ruth forced a smile.

Dr. Tony Daněk, as he introduced himself, thought it better to stay with Ruth on the slopes in case she made the knee worse and later came with Ruth and Lydia back to the hotel to meet Beatrix and Edward. They all sat in the lobby sipping hot red wine with lemon and cinnamon, the local speciality, and to answer Edward's polite questions the doctor said, "I know the local customs; I was born near these mountains. I studied medicine at the King Charles University in Prague. Now I am serving the compulsory year in the military hospital there."

When leaving, Tony asked Ruth if he might ring her up in Prague next week. She hesitated but did not want to be rude, as he was so polite, and gave him the telephone number.

During Ruth's late teens she had met some boys. They seemed to like her. She was lively in company, fairly sporting, and friendly and she danced well, but they meant nothing to her. Tony was no boy; he was about ten years her senior. *Too old for me,* she thought, *not very amusing, good figure, yet not a girl's dream of a man.*

He did ring up after Xmas as promised, but Ruth was not sure she wanted to go out with him. He insisted and said he would ring some other time, and Ruth happily forgot about him. Tony rang again some two weeks later, inviting her to the concert of a well-known pianist, Raphael Kubelik (later a famous conductor), and Ruth agreed. Tony met her in the entrance hall wearing the uniform of a first lieutenant of the Medical Corps, with the sabre worn by men of his rank at the time. He looked extremely well, women admired him in the concert hall, and Ruth was impressed, yet uneasy. She noticed his well-tended, fine, aesthetic-looking hands and she thought his voice was agreeable. He did not speak much, and she never heard him laugh—he did not take her dancing and never put his arms around her, as he was a serious man.

They went together to several more performances, the cinema, and picture galleries. He was knowledgeable in many ways. Ruth respected that and appreciated his comments on art in general.

One Sunday they walked in the snow-covered Lesser Town, the old part of Prague. It was bitterly cold, so Ruth suggested, "We'd better go into one of the tearooms."

"I have an epaulette loose on my uniform; I can't take my overcoat off, it'll need a few stitches. Let's stop at my place; it's just about ten houses down this cobbled street. I expect you can sew," he said, smiling briefly. Ruth burst into laughter, because he doubted her ability.

While Ruth was busy stitching the sign of a serpent on the epaulette, Tony made some tea. They drank it in silence. Then to Ruth's dismay and without a word, Tony began to kiss her, taking her clothes off. She resisted strongly. *What have I done?* she wondered. *He must have misread something.* It was a confusing feeling; she had trusted this decent man. At the same time, inexperienced as she was, she did not want to seem a prude. First she thought it was a mock fight, only there was no fun or tenderness in his action, no talk of love. All he said was, "Calm down and don't be childish."

Ruth did not know precisely what to expect, how to cope with such a situation, as it had not been on the curriculum of the girls' schools she had attended. There was a brisk professionalism about the whole act. He tended to give her instructions; it was so humiliating. Her first thought was to try to run away—perhaps by instict of self-preservation—but she was numb all over, overwhelmed with fright at his strength. She was handled and pressed by a man for the first time. Her stillness meant to him her acquiescence. She was mesmerised, cold, obtuse, as if this were happening to someone else; it all seemed so ominous. Suddenly it was all over, like an operation. The pallor and pain passed, just as when Ruth had had her eardrum perforated.

Tony was not brutal, only so matter-of-fact. Wounded, Ruth hurried into the bathroom to hide her tears, the shock of shame, and the blood on her silk slip.

An empty feeling followed—now she expected a badly needed reassurance. She hadn't really known what sex was, let alone being attacked like this. She had always believed it was something very romantic, gentle, and important.

Ruth faced Tony with her eyes still wet and was in for another shock.

"You have hurt me!" she uttered.

"That's what is called deflowering—nothing to it," Tony said, lighting a cigarette on his way to the bathroom. She sat there feeling guilty and miserable and thought tearfully, *This seduction was certainly not out of a storybook*; deflowering, *what a dreadful word that is. How am I to react? Our relationship is in earnest now,* she assumed. *After this no one else will have me—now I have to marry him. He is more mature than I—can I trust him? What actually is happening to me? Maybe I am exaggerating?*

Ruth could hear the gushing of the shower. It stopped, and she hurried to get dressed. Tony did not help her, and she was unable to just brush it all away. Finally he noticed how awkward Ruth felt.

"Virginity has no value. Everything was quite normal for the first time; you should not be so shy." What a cynical thing to say to her.

"What shall I say to my mother?" she asked, worried.

"Nothing just now, perhaps later," he answered abruptly.

Surely I can leave it to him. He is an educated man; he'll be honest, she kept telling herself.

After this discreditable event, Tony stopped taking Ruth out. He only wanted her to come to his place. Naturally she was offended, yet she considered herself his fiancée from now on and asked, "What are your plans when your military service is over?"

Tony did talk widely about it; obviously Ruth was not included in his future, and she thought it beneath her dignity to ask. She assured herself, *He'll come round.*

Tony had bought tickets for the last concert of the season some time ago, so once again they went out together. Ruth looked forward to it—the Czech Philarmonic Orchestra, directed by V. Talich, would play Dvořák's *Slavonic Dances,* Ruth's favourite. She wanted to be smart and wore her new black silk dress with a large white organdy collar, which suited her shoulder-length dark hair. The concert was impressive, and she would have liked to talk about it, but he had made no comment and escorted her to a nearby restaurant, where Beatrix and Edward were waiting for them. Tony declined to come in but left her by the door.

"Where did you leave the doctor?" wondered Beatrix.

"Actually, he left me. He vanished like a shadow by the entrance." Ruth laughed about it but knew Tony had a guilty conscience.

"Not very civil of him," Edward said, frowning.

* * *

Two months later, Ruth told Tony she had missed her period. He didn't look alarmed but said quite casually, "That does occur sometimes; just wait a little longer."

He is the doctor. I must trust him; it'll be all right, Ruth thought. Soon she felt unwell and ran to her old doctor, who had known her since she was little. It was not all right!

The old doc confirmed her suspicions and asked her about the man in her life, so she told him tearfully that he was a doctor himself but was in no hurry to take care of her.

Ruth told Tony the facts and added, "I have to tell my mother. We have to get married; I am definitely not having an illegitimate child. What am I to do?"

"How annoying." He heaved a sigh and thought it better to let her get rid of the emotional storm. He abashed her and used chilly politeness to bring her sulks to an end. She was quite capable of blowing up the affair out of all proportion. *Give her time; it should put her in a more sensible frame of mind,* he thought. He never mentioned their next date; she had to contact him.

Ruth was getting nervous but thought a few days would make no difference. When she insisted, Tony gave her his answer: "I am not taking for my wife someone who visited my place so casually and willingly; besides, I am not ready to marry anybody. There is nothing I can advise you to do."

Ruth was appalled; there was not a kind note in his voice—now she was not good enough. Speechless, she left in haste, stumbling down the cobbled street as if drunk. The only thing she could do was run back to her old doctor, who now understood his young patient was in real trouble.

"I am going to recommend someone to help you, but first I must speak to your mother," the doctor said with a frown.

Ruth had to tell her mother, which took all her courage. Beatrix was shocked by the way her daughter had been treated by such a seemingly decent man and could not believe it. Concerned, she 'phoned Tony, but he was not there; he had moved to the barracks. He was not available at the hospital either.

"Leave a message please . . . please ring later," the nurse kept saying.

The coward was hiding. Beatrix wanted to go and see Tony's superior officer—only that would have exposed her daughter.

It was the first time in her life Ruth really hated someone. She cursed herself and Tony, went to a private sanatorium, and had a curettage. At that time she suffered a breakdown.

Ruth was on tenterhooks; she could not calm down. Her recovery was slow; she felt bitter and thought it unjust to be put in such a state. If only Tony had shown the slightest interest, 'phoned, sent flowers—there was no sign of him. He had seen many women hanging helplessly in the stirrups, trembling, covered in cold sweat, being scraped just because some irresponsible man had wanted his pleasure—Ruth was just one of the many women.

At first Beatrix had little compassion for Ruth; she thought she should have been more cautious—not as naïve as Beatrix herself had been at Ruth's age. She expected more from Ruth thanks to the education she had been given. At the same time, Beatrix had to admit that while she was solving her own problems she had never thought of giving her daughters some warning about men, and so she blamed herself.

Ruth had to go through the humiliation of it all, but thanks to her mother and the old doctor, she was able to afford the mercy of anaesthetic for the worst part, at least.

She never forgave Tony for being so cagey and not caring whether or not she ended up dead in some back street. His term of service at the military hospital was over, and as he had planned, he left to take up a post of registrar in a provincial hospital and forgot Ruth existed. Devastated more morally than physically, Ruth was gathering her strength and stopped curling up like an injured cat. This was the time when she became closer to her mother, who for the first time talked to Ruth about her own childhood and why she had become so fond of Edward Schwarz, who—like herself—came from a troubled family. He had been devoted to his meek mother, Emily. He had watched her wince each time his father entered the room, but he had been unable to help her. He had confided this with sadness to Beatrix, and this had made them very close.

"Do you remember your Grandpa Emanuel when we visited him with Carl?"

"Yes, I had to lift up my hands and hold the flowers high—he was so tall and did not bend down to kiss me."

"My father was very upright till old age, handsome, and rather regimental. As a master printer, he was well read and intelligent. Carl made the best possible impression on him, as he showed a good knowledge of literature. Grandpa's room had bookshelves on all the walls. They discussed literature over the coffee and cake and didn't bother about the rest of us.

"His coldness was understandable, as he had his share of problems to overcome. My mother, Milena, was a very beautiful, but delicate, daughter of a photographer. She was only twenty years old when she died giving birth to your Uncle Albert and me. It must have been heartbreaking to lose her and be left with baby twins. A great deal of bereavement occurred in his family when he was young—he lost all four of his elder brothers in the 1870 Austrian war.

"There was no time for mourning. Grandpa Emanuel had to remarry quickly, and he chose my mother's cousin Anna, who was kind, cheerful, and capable. She took good care of us and used to sing all day while working in the house. Anna later had a daughter, Sidonie, but still loved and cared for all of us equally."

"I didn't realise that Aunt Sidonie is only your half-sister." Ruth was surprised to hear all this.

"Yes. But to continue, unfortunately, that was not the end of your grandpa's troubles. Anna died of cancer five years later. Now, at the age of thirty-five, Grandpa Emanuel was twice widowed. With the three of us, he could not waste much time with grief. He soon married Agnes, a twenty-seven-year-old, dour, strict countrywoman, who became our legendary 'evil stepmother.'

"Grandpa earned good money but wanted no more children. Maybe this was what made Agnes so bitter. He needed her to run the household smoothly and couldn't be bothered with her stubbornness. He hated domestic quarrels, so he had to give in, to keep the peace in his house, and left everything to her. We children were not allowed in the living room. We had our meals in the kitchen, did our homework there, and slept all together in a small room."

"Wasn't he a misogynist, Mummy, very selfish, too?" remarked Ruth.

"Well, you can find them in every generation, as you know. We seldom have a chance to be alone like this and talk. What I want you to know is that when I was in trouble I had no mother to go to. With my Edward at the front somewhere, I was on my own. So you see, now you can understand everything."

"Please, do go on before Edward comes. He is ever so discreet about me being unwell, and I don't want to deprive him of your company."

"Agnes immediately put us children to work. Albert had to bring coal and do the harder work in the house—we girls had to sew, knit, and help in the kitchen. There was no play after school, just duties or punishment. A piece of cake, an apple, that was reward enough.

"For the summer holidays we were lucky to have our Granny Krasl, our maternal grandma. She was the widow of the photographer. With her in the country, we enjoyed plenty of freedom and we were loved by everybody, including the old dog, Wachtel. The fruit in the garden and orchard and wild fruit in the woods was plentiful, and we felt as free as larks."

"I think I remember visiting Grandma Krasl when I was small. There was an armchair no one was allowed to sit on, and beside it a side table with many pipes no one was allowed to touch—they had belonged to the late Grandpa Krasl."

"You remember correctly—that was always taboo; only Wachtel had the privilege to use the armchair. But Agnes soon put a stop to these holidays as well."

"My twin brother, Albert, was not very strong at fourteen, yet he was sent to work as a live-in apprentice, to a grocer—in fact, this was slavery. There he remained until he turned eighteen, when he enrolled in the then Austrian army in 1915. His right arm was crippled by a stray bullet. He was rewarded with a medal and a job as a civil servant. He married the sparkling Julia; they live in Hradec and have a son, Albert Junior."

"And what did you do, Mummy? Did you stay in school?"

"No, I was also a live-in apprentice in a sweetshop. Agnes wanted us out of the house. I always wished to be a nurse; I went to evening classes until I became one. Once more I asked my father for help, when I was expecting you. But Grandpa Emanuel sent me to the 'Jew.' Grandpa Morice didn't want to hear of me either, as Grandma Emily told you.

"It was only the clever Sidonie who was sent to a commercial college. She worked in a solicitor's office and left only after she married Rudy, a bank clerk, who soon left her and her daughter, Olga. They live in Moravia, as you know.

"Your own life is now much more important. You have to forget this unfortunate, ugly episode as soon as you possibly can, leave it all behind, and never speak about it again."

Beatrix left Ruth to rest and think about it. From now on Ruth was determined to do as dear Camille used to advise: “I’ll keep my stocking seams straight and remain averse to men.”

8

As mentioned previously, Air France had accepted Ruth, and overjoyed, she started to work at the office for a time. She befriended a jolly half-French girl, Marianne Marat. They both were chosen to go for a training course in London—Croydon—to become qualified stewardesses. As they walked the first day across the tarmac wearing brand-new uniforms, they passed an American crew.

"Look, the new broads," said one pilot.

"Yeah. The tall one has a lot of front," said the other and winked at Ruth, who blushed.

"You'll have to get used to that," remarked Marianne, laughing.

When finally Beatrix married her beloved Edward in September, Ruth was in England and could not come to their wedding at the Old Town Hall of Prague. She sent her congratulations from London and wrote further:

> . . . I am happy in England, as always, but very busy; we don't get much free time. There are, again, many Scandinavian colleagues as well as girls from all the Central European countries; it all sounds rather easy, but I wonder how I shall cope in one of those Dakotas . . . I should like to ask you if I may go on using Carl's name; in fact, it is not worth changing; once married, I shall get another name anyhow. . . .

Beatrix recognized, in this, Carl's influence; how tactful and diplomatic Ruth had learnt to be.

* * *

Ruth loved her first job and the people around it. The French pilots were such a jolly lot—they called her "the flying squirrel" because she was quick, had a pointed nose and dark eyes, and would not be easily caught. The less polite ones would remark, "Ruth, she's a touchy one." Maybe, they thought, it was stupidity or some retarded adolescence; in fact, it was severe neurosis and for years to come no one could as much as touch her. The slightest sign of a sexual advance repelled her. This often wrecked her pleasure in dancing. She loved to go to the popular tea dances in London on her days off or in evenings in Paris when the crew had to stay overnight. The tango was her favourite dance, and she was very good at it, too, but if her partner pressed her unnecessarily close, she resented it. The young Englishmen were definitely better behaved than Frenchmen.

Ruth found life in London relaxed, the people friendly. Her English colleagues were very kind. They would take her to their homes in the country for the weekend and make their brothers take her out; it was as if nobody had a single worry.

The atmosphere was not quite so relaxed in Paris. There Ruth often had to spend her free evening alone at the airport accommodation as there was no escort or party to go to. It was better to have a free afternoon and be on a flight to Prague in the evening. This way Ruth could explore the beauty of the French capital and stop at Le Printemps to buy pure silk stockings. They were cheaper there than in London and were better quality than in Prague; what a problem for a girl. She went through quite a few of them in a week.

It seemed that the clouds gathering in neighbouring Germany caused an uneasy atmosphere in France; not so much in England. In the Sudetenland, there were a few Nazis, but they were seen as troublemakers. Everybody felt quite safe until the unfortunate conference in Munich, September 30, 1938.

* * *

The years with Carl had been a child's paradise for Ruth and later for Lydia, but they must have been a sacrifice for Beatrix. She was not unhappy—Carl was too good to her for that—it was just that her heart was not in that marriage. Her daughter knew nothing about the period during which her mother had to solve her marriage problems. There was no space left for Ruth; besides, she was abroad most of the time and did not know how absorbed her mother was in it all. It must have been a reasonably calm sort of aftermath, financially well secured by Edward, who worshipped her.

* * *

Ruth had a short holiday from the Dakotas, which she spent at Edward's house in the circle of her "new family." Beatrix was now forty-one and her happiness was obvious; they walked along the banks of a small river* under the acacia trees. Lydia was singing to the marching, and they all joined in. Beatrix looked at her girls wearing identical dresses, both pretty, one blonde, the other dark, one with a beautiful soprano voice, the other with the ability to speak three foreign languages. Gradually, they all learnt to get on well with each other; even Carl appreciated what Edward did for the two girls.

When Lydia graduated "with excellence" from the teachers' training college, Edward sent her to the conservatory of music. He bought her a Steinway grand piano and hired a teacher, who was to improve Lydia's voice. He invited a visiting tenor from the Berlin Opera to give a private concert with Lydia in their home—the windows shook and clattered at the high notes, and Edward was proud of her.

Edward respected and loved Beatrix; he spoiled them all. When he took his "Drei Mädel Haus" to the theatre or a concert, he wanted them to be well dressed and presented them proudly to his friends and acquaintances. Ruth knew him only as a calm man who never raised his voice and never laughed excessively; he was always dignified.

The winters in Prague can be severe. One day, Ruth was waiting for Edward in his office, as they were going to choose a fur coat for her. She was surprised what a strict director he was, giving orders to his clerks in all directions in an energetic, nearly military manner. She hardly recognized him.

At the furrier's Edward was so generous Ruth had to stop him or he would have bought her a mink. She chose a grey astrakhan trimmed with suede and then she pointed to a matching handbag and gloves. The shop assistant said: "This is the most expensive in the shop."

---

*A tributary of the River Vltava (Moldau).

Edward laughed gently, when Ruth backed away from it, and said with some pride, "That says something about your good taste—you can have it."

When Aunt Sidonie's husband left her, Edward helped to open a beauty salon for her. He financed his brother, Richard, and his wife, Rachel, when they went to Chile. He gave money to Otto, his only friend and solicitor, when he left for the United States. He cared for his nephew, Victor, after his eldest brother, Oscar, died. Edward wanted everybody to be secure; no wonder that Beatrix worshipped him as he did her.

This idyl did not last for long. Hitler was getting ready to invade Austria and Czechoslovakia and made no secret about it; it is mentioned in his book *Mein Kampf.*

After the Munich Conference,* September 30, 1938, the borderland (Sudetenland) of Czechoslovakia was occupied by Nazi Germany. Many people fled from there, especially the Jews. The famous spa Karlsbad, together with many more, like Marienbad, Francesbad, Teplitz, and others, was lost. People panicked to get inside the republic to stay with whichever relative or friend would have them. They lost their property, jobs, everything. But for a short time it was safe in Prague and Vienna.

* * *

Ruth was working in the offices of Air France, as well as alternating with two colleagues as an air hostess. She

---

*Neville Chamberlain's peace mission.

made many friends but still was known as a touchy girl. She was not provocative, coquetry was unknown to her, yet she attracted the wrong men. Perhaps because she had a striking gait. "She walks like a queen," the pilots said as she passed them.

In January, a group of them went to the usual afternoon tea dance. Marianne Marat, the half-French girl, meant to bring her brother as Ruth's partner, but he had something better to do. Marianne came with her fiancé, the rich and simple son of a butcher whom, to Ruth's dismay, Marianne later married. With them came the thirty-three-year-old Mr. Stein.

"Sorry, Ruth, change of partners. This is Herbert, our new neighbour from Karlsbad. He also can dance, I guess," said Marianne with her usual gesticulations.

"Yes, I can—hello, Ruth—but not the minuet; do you mind?" Herbert had a cute smile; in fact, he was charming and witty. He danced as if he were carrying Ruth around the dance floor, and she thought he must have invented ballroom dancing.

Herbert represented several foreign car companies in Karlsbad, but his business had had to be abandoned. For the time being he had nothing to do. He never left Ruth's side, and each day she had to be in Paris Herbert sent her a card, mostly with some very funny remarks. He met her with flowers at the Prague airport, no matter what time of day or night she arrived. He noticed her habit of keeping her hands tightly fisted. He would take her hand, hold it in his, and, after unclenching it gently, kiss her palm.

As they were leaving the pilots' canteen, one pilot remarked rather loudly, "Here comes the touchy one—how can her bones be so beautifully arranged that you can't see any?"

Ruth blushed; she had become overcautious.

"The chap is right; you needn't lose your girlish smile over it." Herbert took her elbow and they walked out of the canteen.

They spent all their free evenings in February out together, dressed up for balls and fancy dress parties, and danced the Lambeth Walk in nightclubs. Some afternoons they sat and talked for hours in one of the many fine *patisseries,* eating cream cakes. On one occasion there was a cherry on top of Ruth's cake but not on Herbert's, so she gave it to him.

"I shall set the stone in gold as a souvenir of your good heart." He stirred his coffee and laughed.

In March Ruth was assigned to fly a group of thirty small, bewildered Jewish children to London—a whole orphanage was to be taken over by the Jewish Refugee Committee. A doctor and several nurses waited for them in Croydon. It was a hard day, and Ruth had to take a late night flight back to Prague (which at the time took four hours). Wearing only her navy blue uniform with the signs of winged Hippocampe, she was cold.

Again, Herbert was faithfully waiting for her. He understood Ruth perfectly, even when she was tired and miserable. He had such a soothing influence on her and could make her smile anytime. It was in the small hours of a frosty morning, but he was there to take her home. When he saw her shivering in the mist, he took his usual grin off his face, covered her shoulders with his trench coat, and said, "Hot lemon tea first; now give me your hands—they are ice cold." He opened her palm, kissed it, and put in it a thin golden chain. An acorn was hanging on it, made from the cherry stone set in a golden cup.

"Die Morgengabe," he said with a cute grin, "because it is morning."

"It is so sweet of you to be here—even if you did not bear gifts," Ruth said tearfully.

"Don't cry, please, or I'll bawl in sympathy. You are my hobby—I never had a hobby before."

Ruth was still so reserved, he sensed that she was not ready for any intimacy and never tried to seduce her. That morning she hugged him with happiness and relief that she could kiss a man at all.

"You are my hobby, too," Ruth whispered.

* * *

Herbert often picked Ruth up at her home; her parents both liked him. He was very courteous to Beatrix, often bringing her flowers or chocolates, and paid her and Ruth compliments. When Ruth was ready he joked, "Smart, isn't she? Does she get herself a new outfit and a new boyfriend every spring?" He also took her to meet his parents, and Ruth found out that Herbert had inherited his charm from his father, who must have been worried, in their precarious situation, yet was quite optimistic. They talked about going to Palestine. They planned to send Herbert first and follow him as soon as he got settled somewhere. Herbert kept holding Ruth's hand during the visit.

"Would you go with me, Ruth as my wife, I mean?" he asked—suddenly.

That was rather an embarrassing surprise. It was a long time since Tony, but even now Ruth was untrusting and insecure; it was too sudden.

"Herbert will have to discuss this with my parents when the time comes," she said to prevent more talk on the subject in front of his parents.

* * *

The Germans invaded the rest of Czechoslovakia on March 15, 1939. Herbert was forced to flee the country quickly and illegally, which was too dangerous for his parents. He left immediately on an illegal ship from the port of Bratislava on the Danube to the Black Sea and on to Palestine. He sent Ruth a card from every port when they anchored, which she shared with his sad parents.

In April it was Herbert's birthday. Ruth spent it in Grandma Emily's garden, crying; she didn't even try to console her. Ruth's relationship with Herbert was too brief and too intense; they were inseparable; it was bound not to last. He was lost to her.

At long last a letter came from Haifa describing the horrors of the voyage—the mice, bad food, typhoid, the dead. They had to swim by night to the shore, with more deaths, and lost their luggage on the ship, which never came into the port. The well-known problems in Palestine at the time followed.

"Please, don't tell my parents about all this; they would be distressed. I only want them to know that I am safely in a camp," Herbert wrote Ruth.

When the war broke out, Herbert, with other Czech Jews, enlisted in the British army. The war was by then raging everywhere, and Ruth got no more news from him.

9

The secure period of the twenty-year-old Republic of Czechoslovakia ended, and its people suffered great hardship. Their second president, Dr. Eduard Beneš, and his government went into exile in England, where Jan Masaryk was the Ambassador to the Court of St. James at the time.

Hitler occupied Poland, and when World War II broke out, Air France closed down their offices in Prague, took all their aircraft with the French staff on board, paid off the Czech staff, and left them to their destiny.

At first it seemed not to be too bad—gradually, however, people had to live under considerable stress. Edward's bank was taken over by a *Treuhänder* under German management, and he was dismissed. The stock exchange was closed. They started to confiscate Jewish property. Edward put everything in Beatrix's maiden name and divided the shares between her and the girls. He had much forethought, and even the telephone was now in his wife's name. Indeed, later the authorities did disconnect the telephones in Jewish households.

"Now they take from Jews; then it will happen to everybody who owns something," Edward said. (He did not live long enough to see this, which did happen when the communist regime took over in 1948.) He also said to Ruth, "You are not too busy now; start to learn Russian." She went to the classes until they were closed down, too.

The Czechs were not anti-Semitic in general; they just distanced themselves from what the Nazis did, and the Czech puppet government was powerless. The order came that no Jew was to be seen in public without a yellow star sewn on his coat, as it was in Germany—punishment was prison. (That was why Edward was later unable to attend the weddings of either of the girls.) Beatrix protected her husband from being exposed to insults wherever it was possible, ready to bear this cross with him.

Meanwhile, Lydia grew into an accomplished opera singer and was engaged as an understudy. Her velvety soprano voice was well suited for the lyrical roles in the operas by Dvořák, Janáček, and Smetana. The glamour of the stage fascinated her, and she could not wait to become a prima donna.

Ruth was sad to have lost the Dakotas and that the future of her country was so bleak. She took a job at a travel agency, which was not very interesting but decent enough for the time being. She had to accompany groups of old people to the few spa resorts left open in Moravia. When winter came, she had the ski parties' transport to take care of. The Giant Mountains being in the occupied territory, they had to go to the lower foothills of South Bohemia for weekends. Ruth had never been there herself and also she was just an average skier, but this was the type of courier she was.

10

Ruth sold a skiing weekend to a young sportsman whom she did not particularly notice at the agency. He turned out to be very helpful when she lost her way, struggling in the darkness and snow to find the chalet. She had dropped her ski gloves in the process. The young man, Peter Smolik, went a mile back to look for them, in vain.

They all arrived at the chalet cold and hungry and enjoyed the hot meal. Peter ordered only a glass of lemon tea and took out of his rucksack bread and sardines. *A poor student,* Ruth thought. *He has such large, rough hands—a farmer's son, perhaps?*

Peter showed kind interest in Ruth's feeble skiing ability and gave her advice on safer skiing. He joined her ski groups most weekends.

On Christmas Day he made a surprise visit to her home.

Ruth's mother left him waiting in the hall and called, "Some boy named Peter, do you know him?"

He had come to wish Ruth Merry Xmas personally and give her a beautiful pair of white leather ski gloves. It was not only a nice gesture, but also an expense, which he most probably could not afford. Ruth was touched by it and agreed to go skating with him on Boxing Day. Again, a sport she was not very good at. Peter was patient with her just as he was on the slopes.

They saw a great deal of each other after that, and

very often they used to hold long conversations on the 'phone in French or English. His mum could not understand, so she would stop him if she was around.

Peter did not like the old-fashioned name Ruth. He called her "Grey Puss," as she wore the grey astrakchan fur coat Edward had given her two winters before. Peter was a modest young man in every way, and whenever they went out together they went "dutch."

Ruth had not used her shorthand since she left college. She meant to leave the travel agency soon, so she enrolled in evening classes to brush up on her shorthand. Peter enrolled with her. They studied together and during the breaks they shared her favourite chocolate bar, which he bought for them.

Soon Ruth started to work in a bank as secretary to the director of personnel, a lawyer who was a stickler for punctuality, which was not Ruth's best asset.

"This morning, Miss Potocky, I walked slowly behind you watching your high heels tapping on the pavement, to give you the chance of reaching the office before me," he often teased her. "Please, Miss Potocky, marry this boyfriend of yours, or else he will make a hole in the pavement waiting for you in front of the bank."

Peter was persistent. They went for Sunday outings, riding, swimming, or taking the old, slow train out into the country. The half-empty carriages had only wooden benches. Peter offered her "first-class travel," sitting on his knees. He was so calm and serious for his age, just six months' difference between them. Most important of all, he made no advances or attempt to have sex.

Ruth was so obviously in need of being cherished, she put much faith in Peter. Any more disappointment would be too painful. He used to listen patiently to her talking about her troubled past—about Tony and the short-lived romance with Herbert. Peter spoke about two of his past girlfriends. They discussed the problem of Ruth's mother being married to a Jew. Peter's opinions were reasonable and he was tolerant. He waited patiently to take Ruth home from her ballet classes and kissed her good night—they never had a single tiff.

Peter could not finish his engineering studies. Since the students' unrest, the Germans had kept the universities closed. When Peter's commercial course ended he planned to get a job until it was possible to resume his studies. In spring, they walked through one of the many parks in Prague. Peter paused.

"Look at the beautiful chestnut blossoms—when the ripe chestnuts start falling, we will get married." He meant it. The romance had developed rather rapidly for Peter, reluctantly for the hesitating Ruth.

"First, we must find a 'basket' for 'Grey Puss' and me to sleep in—then you must come with me to the Moravian church to see my old teacher, the vicar. I would like you to take some Bible lessons with him and join the church. It is the family tradition. We will be 'dropped from the pulpit' [the reading of the banns] and get married there," he added.

As much as Ruth disliked churches (she had had too much of them in the orphanage) and was indifferent to any religion, she went, so as not to offend Peter. By now she would have missed his company, his sincere friendship, and the knowledge he had of all sorts of subjects. Peter kept surprising her—his secret was that he was able to remember all he read, even last week's newspapers. She learned from him, and he never bored her.

Ruth had enjoyed her ballet classes ever since she was small. She even travelled with an opera group and performed in the ballet sequences and acted as an extra. On one occasion her group was putting on a performance at a dinner-dance given by the Auto Club. She asked Peter to come and he agreed, saying, "I wonder if I can still get into my dinner jacket?"

Ruth took it as a joke. It was the custom in those days to wear dinner jackets to a dinner dance, but the students or younger men would wear dark suits. Peter picked her up, and as the weather was bad, he was wearing a raincoat. They arrived at the Auto Club and met Jan by the cloakroom. Ruth had met no one from his family so far and none of his friends.

"This is my brother—Miss Potocky." Peter presented Jan, a tall, very handsome young man who was wearing a perfect dinner jacket, and so was Peter.

Jan took Ruth to the table; Peter followed. There were the men's parents, and she was introduced. She made a great effort to cover her shock—the blond lady in her forties, bedecked in jewellery like a Xmas tree and wearing a white fox wrap was Peter's mother; the respectable, bespectacled gentleman, his father. The conversation was rather strained at their table. Luckily, Jan asked her onto the dance floor; he spoke about his interrupted studies at the law school.

Peter was not much of a dancer, as he had no sense of rhythm. Jan was more popular and had many more girls to dance with, so Ruth was stuck at the table politely answering all sorts of questions for *le maître.* Finally, she had to go and change for their little show, in which she had a short solo—"Persian Market," by Ketelbey.

After Ruth returned to the table, three or four young men asked her for a dance at once. *How is it they did not notice me before? What do they expect of me?* She was not a showgirl; they were just an amateur group. *Isn't Peter going to stop them, protect me?* He took no notice whatsoever.

Once more she was to endure Peter's parents' scrupulous examination. They were staying in a small spa not far from Prague and asked Peter and Ruth for a weekend. There was no petrol for private cars during the war, so they went by train. *Le maître* was in the best of his many moods and rather extravagant. He was a good linguist himself and was impressed with Ruth's French and the rest of her education. She was more self-confident this time. Also, she was well trained in good manners, which was approved of by his wife.

On their way back to Prague, Peter was pleased, but Ruth still felt his mother's observant eye, which took in every detail of her appearance.

"They like you; now we can proceed. I shall go and see your folks next Sunday. We can fix the date and ask if it is all right at the church," Peter said. Ruth could not stop his enthusiasm. "Aren't you rushing things? You didn't tell your parents. Mine are in for a surprise; your job is not certain, we have no flat yet, and I need a special permit, documents, coupons for a wedding dress, and extra rations for the reception."

Peter was obstinate, as he always was when he wanted something for himself. At the time it was Ruth—or was he feathering his own nest and looking for a chance to get out of the snob's straitjacket he disliked at home? Ruth wondered.

Beatrix was warned in time that Peter was coming for Sunday lunch. He brought her flowers, but there was no engagement ring for Ruth. He made a good impression on Edward, who said, "He is too young for you, intelligent, yet professionally unfinished, but he seems sincere enough. I believe, given time, he can make it."

Edward asked his solicitor to make some discreet enquiries about the lawyer Smolik. The answer was that he was a millionaire!

Beatrix always observed how men ate, while Ruth was sensitive to men's voices. "He certainly does not look like a member of a wealthy family, and he ate abstractedly," Beatrix remarked.

Now the real trouble started. Peter's parents did like Ruth, yes, but not as their daughter-in-law. No wonder Ruth felt so uneasy about Peter's parents, and each occasion they met proved to be no exception. Now they fumed; there were arguments, threats to Peter, tears, and awkward silence. Peter's mother realised she could not stop her son from marrying Ruth but ordered that no member of the family was to go to the wedding.

Peter accepted a job as a technician in a factory. They rented a small third-floor flat in a smart part of Prague, and went on with the preparations.

Edward assured Ruth, "The Smoliks will cool down eventually."

Ruth took Peter to tea with the wise "agony aunt," Bertha, who was famous in the family for giving good advice to the young members. She folded them both into her ample bosom, made them eat her tasty *Kugelhupf,* hot chocolate with lashings of whipped cream, and watched them discreetly. Her firm verdict was: "Peter is no match for you. He'll never make you happy. He'll waste his intelligence and education and make no money; he has no respect for money."

Bertha had seen Peter only once, so Ruth didn't believe her vision, which she didn't think was accurate.

Edward was a modern, assimilated Jew. He never even went to a synagogue, but he was in the Jewish birth register, which was in German hands. The order to wear the yellow Star of David applied to him. At the time Ruth was to marry Peter Smolik, Edward was already a persecuted person and was in no position to be able to protect his daughter from the slanderous insults the Smoliks had thrown on her and her family. He couldn't possibly take Ruth to the church. He said to her with a sad smile, "You shall have to go through a difficult phase—it's called life, and I can't help you there."

Ruth would have loved to have Carl, still her dear father, there to give her away. He always promised his daughters to dance with them on their wedding day, but he could not with either of them. It would not have been fair to Edward, who had to stay at home and who did see to it that they had a luxurious reception in spite of the war. So a distant uncle took Ruth to the church and Edward paid for the rings, the cars, the flowers, the photographs—all of it—and as the young couple was leaving, Edward asked the groom if he had enough money on him. In fact, for the honeymoon he had very little, so Edward paid for the honeymoon as well. He gave Peter an expensive camera with all the extras. There was no wedding present from her "poor-rich" husband, nor from his absent folks. Only Rose, Peter's grandmother, sat alone in the back of the church; she did not come to the reception. She knew Ruth from her visits to the farm when, with Peter, they used to stop there on their bicycles, the thirsty couple.

The newly marrieds left in a *fiacre* (horse and carriage cab) for the station and travelled to the lower mountains by train. The hotel was modest, to say the least, no bridal suite. Rain was coming down in buckets all the time in September. They spent the days walking in the wet, foggy forest, ate on rations (restaurants were not excluded), and spent their evenings listening to the gurgling of rainwater down the drain. There wasn't even a radio. To keep warm they both read from one book in bed.

Ruth got over the inexperienced, clumsy sex that seemed so loving on the honeymoon, when it is the right time for it and nothing else matters. She did not think it was a failure. She was young and ready to overcome all adversities, willing to adjust and accept Peter. After all, he was to be part of her future; she learned to tolerate him and wanted a child.

After that short stay they travelled by train back to Prague to their new home, for which Edward had paid the rent for a year in advance.

Before their arrival, Beatrix had the flat furnished and ready, complete from carpets to cutlery. The bed and quilts were too short for Peter, who was six feet tall. He brought his own bed and bedding, books, and the rest of his personal belongings and settled in his room with his new hobby—radio making.

Their everyday married life started still in wartime. Peter had an hour's bus ride to the factory and had to leave before 7:00 A.M. Ruth made his sandwiches and left by tram to be in the office at 8:00 A.M. They had to go to bed early and did not go out much. She looked after the household, and Peter spent a lot of time with his hobby. Ruth went to her ballet classes, Peter to his gym and boxing. On weekends they went to pictures; they saw Czech or German films and met friends. The horses had been requisitioned by the German army, so riding was out. Born in the capital, Prague, Ruth loved nature and open-air activities, and so did Peter. One rather cold day she attended his sports club swimming competition, anxiously holding his bathrobe, but he was not chill-prone and hardly ever caught a cold.

Sometimes they visited their respective parents—separately, of course.

Marie, Ruth's illustrious mother-in-law, was quite a snob; she loved to show off. She had expensive tastes in decor and in dress, at times overdoing the furs and jewellery perhaps. In society, she was ornamental but dull, could hardly speak any foreign language, and was largely ignored in the diplomatic circles where her husband loved to move; Ruth wondered where her self-confidence came from.

There was only one person Marie feared and respected—her single sister-in-law, Magdalena Smolik, the formidable doctor of the family. She was the only one who dared to disagree with Marie. Magdalena also detested Marie's reason for declining the invitation to her son's wedding. She wanted to know about her nephew's wife and started to investigate in her own bizarre way. She came to see Ruth in her office; after the interrogated boss was left rigid and flabbergasted, Magdalena turned on poor, surprised Ruth, who had only just met the lady and burst into tears, because much less could make her cry.

"You look miserable, Ruth. Are you all right? Is something wrong with your health?" Magdalena asked.

So Ruth sobbed out, "I am sick early in the mornings and that is all."

Immediately Magdalena made an appointment for Ruth to come and see her at the surgery; she arranged for the obstetrician, the Sanatorium St. Bernard was alerted, the baby's layette was ordered, the names were chosen for the baby, and the christening was organised, so Ruth had no choice but to deliver it.

Magdalena's brother, Frank, no *maître* to her, was actually ordered to stop all this narrow-minded nonsense and accept his son's wife.

"The girl is miserable and that is not good for your first grandchild," Magdalena fumed. This was how she always ordered people about.

When Marie *had* to invite Ruth to tea she, of course, resented the idea and was ready to give the girl a frosty reception. No one could stop her from welcoming Ruth like a skunk at a garden party. She used her lorgnette, sat rigidly at the table, her fingers steepled together, her eyes cold, and remarked succinctly, "You have to behave properly as a member of our family, and if you must have a child, it had better be a boy."

This insult and tears Ruth had to swallow. Peter, her husband, did nothing to stop this humiliating situation. She thought how men are willing to promise to be something they can't possibly be—protective, for instance. No wonder Marie was nicknamed "Czarina" by her husband's staff. She probably counted the silver spoons after Ruth left.

When on a Saturday the time came, Peter had to be called at his sports club, where he always went on Saturdays. He took his wife into the maternity ward and left her there. After seven hours' labour, on Sunday morning Ruth delivered a boy—as she was ordered! Peter didn't come to see them until the afternoon and found Ruth in tears—of course.

"The flower shops are closed; I bought this from a lady's window box," and Peter presented Ruth with a potted geranium.

Magdalena sent a pediatrician to look the baby boy over, and his Grandpa Smolik sent a narrow golden bracelet from his wife's large jewellery collection.

The christening (for some twenty-five people) was

held on a cold February day at the Smoliks' overdecorated residence. War or no war, it was lavish. No one from Ruth's family was invited. No one asked how she felt about it, not even Peter.

Jan was supposed to be the godfather, but now married to a plain but rich girl, he declined, and he was not among the guests. Ruth thought, *What a strange family they are,* but Peter didn't think so and asked his friend Vladimir to do the honours.

Marie was receiving all the congratulations, the flowers, the gifts; she was showing the baby Simon around. Not even the vicar took any notice of Ruth. They all treated her as if she were the nanny. She hated it all and withdrew into the white and gold Louis XIV bedroom and cried over the baby's cot. Her husband, again, did not as much as lift a finger, noticed nothing out of the ordinary, had not a single kind word for his young wife—nothing! The sensitive girl started to doubt him.

Ruth had had to stop working some time ago. They had to live sparingly and she worried about it, but Peter didn't give up any of his pleasures or hobbies and left her to manage. Luckily, Edward saw to it that she had some money of her own, and she was ashamed to admit that she needed more quite badly. Gradually she had to forget the small luxuries; even having her hair done was considered too self-indulgent and she could not pay for any new clothes she would have liked after the pregnancy.

Peter had no idea how to support Ruth or the family and knew she would cope somehow. In vain she longed for his attention and care—which cost nothing—but he would shake her off. Ruth felt like Hedda Gabler when he said, "You are *un caramel collant*—go to see your mum, invite your friends, read, or something." It seemed so long ago when Peter used to tell her, "Your eyes are as sparkling as a child's at a funfair." He had not noticed when and why they had stopped sparkling. He did absolutely what *he* wanted and left her to do whatever was necessary—and that's how it was to be from now on.

Thanks to the war and her marriage, Ruth's promising personality came to nothing.

11

Marie Smolik, nee Vacha, had been born on a large farm in West Bohemia; she was one year old when her father died of tuberculosis and her widowed mother, Rose Vacha, was only twenty-one. She was an energetic, headstrong lady and took over the command of the people on the farm, which she ran with an iron hand. Rose rejected all offers of another marriage, even from the local doctor. "They all see a prosperous farm," she proclaimed. "No, there will never be a stepfather for Marie."

Rose spoilt her daughter, who became the best-looking and the best-dressed of all the girls in the district. She went to a finishing school, where she learned housekeeping, cooking, and sewing—rather a mediocre education, yet Marie was well organised and when, at the age of eighteen, she married the lawyer Smolik, whom she met at a ball in Prague, she was able to run a large household well, with the help of two or three maids, of course.

The family Smolik decided that the best and fairly safest plan for Peter (in 1943–44) would be to live with Grandma Rose on her farm. It was also economical, so Peter left his job, never caring to ask how Ruth, unaccumstomed to such a hard, dull country life, felt about living in the bleak, neglected, uncomfortable farmhouse.

This was *not* the farm in Switzerland! This old-fashioned kitchen was constantly full of flies. The window led onto the courtyard, with a dunghill and a leaking cesspool running across it. There was no garden, just an unkempt orchard behind the barn. No 'phone or radio and no visits from her own folks.

Ruth hardly ever came out of the kitchen, where she had to do the daily catering for six to eight people, and the only help was a fifteen-year-old half-wit daughter of one of the factors, whose aristocratic name was Henrietta. Rose was busy in the fields and barn, Peter with the tractor and threshing machine. They both came home hungry and tired, with no interest or as much as thanks for Ruth, who didn't even have any pocket money—and no time for little Simon.

The silly girl who was supposed to look after the child was useless. She left the pram in the middle of the road and ran away when a car was approaching, gave Simon wild berries to eat and made him sick, and kept hidden for hours sleeping in the hay. Ruth herself was too busy to be able to take the baby walking in the woodlands and fields belonging to the farm. Once she came to help with the hay harvest. Rose wondered where she, the town girl, had learnt to tend the hay so well. Out in the fresh air Ruth felt more as if she were on the Swiss farm.

The country fair was approaching, and Ruth knew how to swathe the curds in a wet cloth to make cottage cheese, with which the traditional Czech cookies are filled, decorated with raisins, some with apples and cinnamon, some with homemade plum preserves and almonds, others with ground poppyseeds, cooked in milk and sugar. There had to be enough cookies for the family and many visitors. When the large kitchen table was full, Ruth had to cover the ironing board with cloth and line them up there.

Everybody loved those cookies looking like little pillows filled with sweetened poppyseeds.

"Hurry, girl!" Rose called. The coal- and wood-heated ceramic oven was as fast as in a bakery, and was situated in a building across the yard. Ruth had to be quick to bring the trays to and from the oven. Dusted with vanilla-flavoured sugar, the extremely tasty cookies disappeared very quickly when served to the guests.

12

While still breast-feeding Simon, who was nine months old now, Ruth became pregnant again. She went to Prague to see her good old obstetrician, whose name was Dr. Stork, very appropriately, and told him tearfully, "I didn't want a baby so soon."

Dr. Stork talked her out of taking some drastic measures, and so did her parents, whom she also visited. They cheered her up with a visit to the National Opera and persuaded her that it would be better for Simon not to be an only child for too long. Her young husband was noncommittal as usual, so Ruth stopped feeding Simon and went on with it.

The father-in-law and Marie would sometimes come for weekends to collect eggs, chickens, rabbits, lambs, vegetables, and logs of wood so that they could enterain in town. In June, Ruth was heavy already and hot; one day she fainted, letting a pile of plates fall on the floor.

When they invited guests, Ruth was excluded from the company. Marie would send her to stay in her room, as she had grown bigger and was not "presentable." Ruth did as she was told but was lonely and miserable, mainly because she had no love or support from her husband; Peter also thought no change, pleasure, or distraction was good for her, but the dreaded too much hard work was.

At least, *le maître* kept many books everywhere. Ruth

would go to bed early and read whilst resting, to prevent her brain from becoming too dull.

On one occasion they were all invited to dinner at a farm in the neighbouring village. It was a mild July evening, and Ruth looked forward to it. She had one decent dress cleverly made for the previous pregnancy, but when she was dressed and ready, Marie said, "Where do you think you are going with your big belly?"

The words were like a tinderbox!

This time Ruth went red in the face: "I am not your maid to be ordered about—I am your son's wife, and in the big belly is his child, so he is not going anywhere either!"

Silence! Peter didn't dare utter a whisper—Ruth was sick of his cowardly dependency. It was her father-in-law who recovered from the shock first and said, "Well, we had better all go."

When they arrived at the friends' farm, the host took no notice of the others. He took Ruth gently down from the carriage, guided her slowly to their summerhouse, looked for the most comfortable deck chair, and put a blanket over her knees, asking if she was warm enough. He served her first, spoke to her with respect, called her madam, and brought freshly picked raspberries with cream especially for her.

There was no way even the phlegmatic Peter and the in-laws could have overlooked the fuss. Back at home, alone, Ruth said to her husband, "That man was not as educated as you are, but he is a gentleman," hoping in vain that Peter might be ashamed of himself.

Marie stayed at the farm to take over the household when Ruth had to go to Prague in time to await the birth. Her doctor advised her not to stay in the country for the birth, and Ruth would not have been able to bear it. Rightly, too, as baby Bernard weighed over eight pounds—

and it was a difficult delivery, again on a Sunday. Peter kindly came to see them when it was all over—no flowers, in August! No gift from grandparents Smolik.

For three weeks after the painful confinement (doctor's orders, confirmed by Magdalena, the family doctor), Ruth was peaceful and comfortable with her parents, who spoiled her and prepared a small reception when Bernard was baptised in the very church where Peter and Ruth had been married three years before. This time Jan and his wife, Draga, represented the Smoliks and Peter's friend Eugen was the godfather—all thanks to Edward, who cared.

Ruth, of course, was pining for eighteen-month-old Simon, who might have been asking for his mummy—it was time to go back to the farm.

It was again Edward who hired a taxi (a rare commodity in wartime) for mother and baby to get them safely to the farm. Ruth did not expect a rapturous welcome; she knew better by now. When she arrived with the model baby Bernard, there was no welcome at all. Marie was all packed and ready to use the car back to Prague, too busy supervising the luggage and baskets of food—with not even a smile for the baby and a kind word for Ruth. Peter ignored her usual tears. The Smoliks stepped into the taxi and were off.

In Ruth's absence, Marie had soon lost patience with the teenage Henrietta and sent her away. A proper, mature maid was there now. She took Ruth upstairs, helping with the baby things. Their room had been left in a mess; the cot was not ready—Ruth had nowhere to put the baby—she was upset.

Hanka, the country woman, was efficient and did everything necessary to calm Ruth down; it was time for breast-feeding. She picked up nappies for washing and went down to the kitchen and was back again with a cup of herb tea (there was no real tea during the war). She was daring, too.

"Your wife is crying upstairs, sir. Aren't you going to talk to her?"

"Nothing I have to say would help; she is just hysterical."

His answer made Hanka shake her head. She became Ruth's right hand and ally.

Ruth doted on her sons, but ever since that day Bernard was her slight favourite. She reproached herself that she had not wanted her Raphael-like cherub. Simon ran to his mother as she was feeding his brother and asked to "drink like this" as well. So she had a lot of explaining to do.

* * *

The harvest was over; with a good maid and less cooking to do, Ruth had more time for the children. It was such a calm, sunny autumn, even Peter joined her for walks with the pram along the meandering brook that was bubbling over rocks down to the river, carrying Simon on his shoulders. The wooded hills were bright with reds and yellows among the dark green conifers.

Three months passed in the daily routine and relative tranquility—then the shock! Before Christmas 1944 Edward was transported to the concentration camp in Terezín and Peter was listed to go to a German labour camp. Even the mighty *maître* could not stop it. This was the most terrible time for everybody.

Edward was anxious not to leave Beatrix in an awkward situation on her own again. He did his utmost to secure her financially and gave instructions to his solicitor. Peter, on the other hand, delivered Ruth to the tender mercies of his parents, together with his children. He was not there to protest, if he had had the guts to do so, when his family decided firmly: the "Jewess" must go!

Ruth was sent back to Prague immediately. Alone, she travelled by train, holding one child's hand, the other on her arm, and a heavy bag. Simon, now twenty-two months old, fell asleep before the train arrived at the station. She had to carry him, too. A passing man helped Ruth to get the pram from the luggage carriage and into the tram. Ruth and the boys arrived exhausted at their unheated flat. The gas stove in the kitchen was the only source of warmth. Only thanks to Rose, who had quickly packed some food for them, the children were now fed and in bed.

Ruth was so tired and frustrated she could not go to sleep. She said each word that came to her mind in four languages, in the sequence she had learned them, like so: "*stůl, der Tisch, la table,* the table; *okno, das Fenster, la fenêtre,* the window; *strop, die Decke, le plafond,* the ceiling; *střecha, das Dach, le toit,* the roof . . . " nearly asleep, "I don't know where my husband is exactly. I wish I was single, infecund, and hidden in the old convent. I am turning into a complete idiot . . . "

* * *

Edward's deportation crashed on Beatrix; she was nearly out of her mind and helpless. Suddenly they were lepers. Ruth had the flu but had to go out to get their rations. She was soon underweight and suffering from her heart's mitral valve insufficiency; little Bernard had pneumonia; but not even Magdalena, the family doctor, would approach them. Sad and lonely, Ruth had to cope on her own using the money left her by Edward.

In spite of the fact that Ruth's maiden name had been Potocky, the persecution spread to her and she was summoned for medical inspection to be sent to a labour camp. The Nazis wanted mainly younger women. The German doctor was the military kind and rather frightening. Ruth did dare to tell him she had a two- year-old child and was still breast-feeding the baby and that there was nowhere to put the children. The doctor squeezed her breast roughly to check, and the milk sprayed him. He was furious but did let her go.

Shortly after Christmas, Bernard's godfather, Eugen, passed by on a cold evening by chance and visited Ruth. He knew nothing of her situation. He found them all in the kitchen and hot water on the stove, as Ruth was going to do the washing by hand. It was the time of the Nazi searches.

"I am afraid because Peter has a very large stock of radio and electrical equipment. They could be suspicious of illegal broadcasting," Ruth said.

"You can expect a search anytime; it would be safer if I take it away." Eugen also got in touch with Simon's godfather, Vladimir, and together they acquired a ration of coal for Ruth.

There was no lift in the house; Ruth had to take the coal up from the cellar bucket by bucket to the third floor and the ashes down. She had to carry up the little food she could buy, the pram, and the children, one by one, up the three floors. Usually one boy was screaming upstairs or the other left still downstairs—or both.

In February the American airaids over the Czech

territory intensified. On the fourteenth, Prague itself was bombed, right across the centre, not military targets, just people's homes. There were many dead and injured. Later this was called a "mistake" by the U.S. command.

Ruth alone was responsible for the lives of their children. Day and night, she took them down to the shelter to protect them against all odds.

Once the children were washed and in bed, Ruth tidied up and could sit down with some mending and rest. The radio was mostly boasting of Nazi victories, the Czech programmes censored; she preferred the silence after the day with noisy children. Often the siren sounded—then she grabbed the bag with coupons, money, a thermos of milk, some food, and nappies, already in it. If the raid was serious, the warden would come for her and help her to carry one of the sleeping boys down to the shelter. He knew she was alone up under the roof, helpless if it caught fire. All clear—Ruth still didn't dare go to bed. She had a permanent feeling of danger.

Granny Rose had to supply Marie's household with food, even with wood. The sullen farmhand took all day by horse and carriage to get to town and back. Secretly he stopped at Ruth's place to leave a small parcel of food and a box of wood for them. He liked Ruth and would never have told Marie about this stop Rose told him to make.

The U.S. Army was approaching from the west, the Soviet one from the East; the Nazis were frantic and dangerous. It was known by the citizens that in the nearby woodlands, where Ruth lived, there were Czech and Slovak partisans hidden. Ruth took bread, cheese, or cooked potatoes in the pram, walked there, and left it under a tree. The partisans would not show themselves, but the food was gone the next day. She would bring some more when she could, and so did other Czechs in the region.

The U.S. general Patton was stopped on the west border of Czechoslovakia when the Yalta Conference decided the Czechs must wait for the Soviets. It took them five more days to get to the unarmed and isolated Czechs. A lot of wasted lives, terrible bloodshed, more death in the camps, ruined treasures and mediaeval buildings, those were the results of it.

The last consignment of Germans in Ruth's district took over her flat on the third floor in order to aim the machine guns at the main road, where the Soviets were fighting for every inch of the streets of Prague. The young German soldiers turned her furniture to face the walls, rolled the carpets away, took the curtains down, and installed their guns in her windows. They only damaged the parquet floor.

Ruth and everybody else from the house were sent to the cellar—they were there for two days and nights. Suddenly, the Germans left. It was all over.

The Soviets came to dismantle the guns and take them away, together with everything else it was possible to steal that was not nailed to the wall. In vain they looked for vodka in Ruth's household.

It was May 1945—the liberators were welcomed, whoever they were. These Soviet soldiers were mostly very young and from remote parts of the USSR. They looked exhausted.

13

The war over at last, people were relaxed and hopeful. Happy were those who had their sons and husbands back home, and many felt compassion for those who were mourning for their loved ones. In the first year of peace, people were not yet divided by their various political parties and different opinions, nor by the economic boom or crisis. The Soviets were allies and for a short time nations were united by relief and peace.

Ruth was glad to see her husband unharmed. He was all right, just rather thin, and had frostbite on his hands and feet. He had certainly undergone a frightful time before the Nazis left the camp; they could have had the hundred men shot before the Americans could reach it, but luckily, they were in too much of a hurry to leave themselves. The freed prisoners marched in groups from the west border of Czechoslovakia in the opposite direction from the departing German troops.

Peter managed to reach the farm and continued by bicycle from there. The German soldiers marching in the opposite direction also wanted to get home safely, but they would still shoot at the smallest provocation.

Ruth had missed him and also she hoped he would share the responsibility for their children with her now. She was tired with the burden of it. Secretly she hoped he would appreciate all she had gone through and love her for it, as she was longing for him to care. But stoicism was one facet of his character that would never change.

His family received him as a hero, and he never mentioned Ruth's merits. She desperately wanted to restore the rapport they had had in the early days before children came, but in vain.

He needed to finish his studies in the shortest possible time now that the universities were reopened and gave her no chance. On the contrary, in order not to be disturbed, he sent Ruth and his sons to spend the summer in a small town some twenty kilometres from Prague up the river Vltava.

The rented rooms were in a house on a hill, situated in the middle of a cherry orchard. They had a balcony with a view of the river and the hills on the opposite side of the valley. It was blissful. Peter came to see them sometimes, not too often, though.

One Saturday, the peaceful house was full of excitement, for the son of the landlady, a Czech pilot serving in the RAF, came to visit his mother. He was now stationed in Germany and had a weekend off. In the car with him came a British army officer with a moustache. All the neighbours welcomed them, chattering in Czech all at once. Ruth said to the British officer in English, "I am afraid none of them speaks English. Please excuse them for being so noisy and excited; they have seen only Russian soldiers so far."

"Oh, good," he said, smiling. "So I shall not be completely lost here." They shook hands. "My name is Kenneth."

"I am Ruth. I was often in London—that is, Croydon Airport—before the war; I worked as an air hostess. I shall be taking my children for a walk this afternoon—you may come with me if you wish, down there to the riverbank."

"Yes. I would like to look around and give my friend the chance to be alone with his family."

The landlady was extremely proud of her son, quite rightly, too. He had been decorated, had such good manners, and looked well. He brought his mother photos of his English wife, Beryl, and son, John, as well as gifts.

Kenneth spent most of the weekend in Ruth's company. He pushed the pram or carried the baby. They sat and talked in the orchard or on the balcony; they could hear the laughter and talk from below. The landlady invited her friends to see her hero, and they drank many a toast to him and his family.

Returning from their walk on Sunday morning, Ruth and Kenneth stopped to get some milk at a farm. Kenneth asked about the strange woman there, the farmer's sister. Ruth told him about her husband, who had parachuted into the nearby woods with other Czechs serving in the Soviet army; he managed to contact her, which was very dangerous. She helped him secretly, but he was caught, tortured, and executed in the fortress of Terezín by the Nazis.

"Now she is mentally disturbed," Ruth informed him.

They met a platoon of Soviet soldiers, all in a pitiable state after a long march. The men were heading for the local football club, which had been transformed into a disinfection and delousing station.

Kenneth was astonished at the state of the soldiers, how exhausted and dirty they looked. They had suffered a great deal on their way to Central Europe across the devastated lands. They had hardly any leave and no news from their families. Often the officers had no evidence of the many casualties; there was no Red Cross in the USSR to speak of.

At each station the Soviet soldiers had a shower, a medical exam, and a clean uniform. The old uniforms were burnt. The soldiers sat in the sun on the platform eating out of tins. (The UNRRA, United Nations Relief and Rehabilitation Administration, organised by the Atlantic Charter, came later.)

One of the Soviet soldiers played "Garmoshka," a small concertina.

"They need little to be happy. By comparison the puffed-up U.S. soldiers are treated like film stars," Kenneth remarked.

The weekend over, Kenneth and his Czech friend had to drive back to their base in Germany.

There was good and bad in all the armies; the U.S. soldiers were not always gentlemen either. The only real gentlemen were in the British army; they came to Prague or Vienna on duty or on leave. An English club was established in Palace Koruna, where they could meet. The Czech soldiers who came back with English wives would also go there. BBW* was founded, and some learnt Czech fast. After she came back to Prague in the autumn, Ruth also became a member and helped with translations for them all.

Some Czech revanchists turned on the remaining Germans, mostly their women and children, and treated them badly. They herded them up and made them walk for miles into former German camps with their crying children, the poor belongings loaded on the prams. Most of the Czechs thought they were punishing the wrong ones.

---

*British Born Wives.

The guilty ones had been long gone, fleeing by cars and aeroplanes. Some said, "So what? The war was their idea."

All this was unnecessary. To end this revanchism, those people were gradually transported back to Germany with the help of the International Red Cross.

While in England and the United States patriotism was encouraged, in the occupied countries it was brutally suppressed, and now it flared up. The daily fear was over and other problems piled up for the survivors.

Edward came back from the concentration camp in Terezín in June 1945, after he had recovered from typhoid in quarantine. He was a wreck of a man, his spirit broken, his health damaged, his money devalued, his shares lost, and with no prospects of work, for his old position was not available. (The stock exchange closed in 1939 and never reopened.)

Ruth's former boyfriend, Herbert Stein, arrived in Prague, still in uniform, with medals. Marked by war, having suffered from malaria, he was not the same man anymore. He was informed that his parents had been deported to a Polish concentration camp,* where they had died in 1942. There was no chance of his getting back his property after lengthy repatriation of the Germans from the Sudetenland—and he did not seem to care. His usual grin and his sense of humour became rather arrogant, his expressions vulgar. He hardly recognised the soignée, smart former stewardess, now neglected, thin, and tired-looking. He ruined her opinion of him by making advances to Ruth, then left to "demob" without saying good-bye. Suffering does not always build a character; mostly it

*Auschwitz.

destroys it. He took with him the best memory she had of him. His gold chain with the acorn was lost together with other valuables when the Soviet conscripts "cleared" Ruth's flat. Later a letter came to say he had followed his sister and her family to Brazil.

There was a parade of Czechoslovakian legions—headed by Field Marshal Montgomery.* Ruth went to see all the brave, proud men, mostly pilots, who had served side by side with the British forces. Herbert was not among them! Those serving with the Soviet army had a parade in Bratislava, the Slovak capital, under the command of Gen. Ludvik Svoboda (later president). There was a general sigh of relief, but no more jubilation.

Like everybody else, during the war Peter and Ruth had been planning what they were going to do when the war ended and the universities opened again. Peter had to finish his already started M.Sc. in engineering, and he wanted Ruth to study medicine and later take over the surgery from the aging Magdalena. For the time being Ruth took private lessons in Latin, necessary for medical school. She found it interesting, but as she already had some exams in modern languages, she thought it more practical to get herself a degree in those. But before she could do this, Ruth had two small children who needed all her time and attention, and by the time the war was over her financial circumstances made it impossible to hire a nanny. So she had to give up her plan, and Peter had underestimated her ever since. He, on the other hand, had all the opportunities and did not use them as he could have done.

---

*September 22, 1945.

Peter resumed his studies at once—and had his degree day before 1945 ended. The whole family was at the ceremony, and Beatrix came with Edward, too. It was all over, he didn't have to wear the yellow star anymore, yet the two sets of parents, now grandparents, still had never met. The nearly three-year-old Simon kept running from one pair to the other and back again, so that after the ceremony they had to be introduced to each other at long last. The celebration was at the Smoliks' residence, but again, Ruth's parents were not invited, which spoiled another important, joyful day for her.

As Ruth watched the beautiful ancient ceremony, proud of Peter, she hoped that one day he'd be amongst the professors. Instead, he remained a lecturer at his school for thirteen years. There he rested on his laurels. As he had been a gifted student, his parents must have had great hopes for him as well. He was wasting his intelligence and his education on his hobbies, which were always more important to him than his career, which Ruth hadn't realised before. In vain she counted on his family's influence, but they didn't have any. Their second son, Jan, was now a lawyer like his father and had married a rich girl. Marie spent her time mostly in bed having difficulties with her menopause, her private gynaecologist in and out of her bedroom.

Peter kept disappointing Ruth more and more; she just had to tolerate his idea of happiness even as they became hard up. She had a few private pupils to whom she gave French lessons, at least until the boys started to go to school.

Unlike Ruth's parents, the Smoliks avoided the attention of the Nazis and kept their many properties. As a solicitor, Frank Smolik had many German clients, some aristocrats among them. He was virtually a collaborator.

Amongst others, he was in a partnership with an Austrian businessman who, accused of sabotage, was arrested with all the Smoliks, sons, cousins, and namesakes. They all spent a chilling week at the Petcheck Palace, the headquarters of the Gestapo in Prague.

This at least could not be blamed on Ruth. She was petrified, as it was in the dangerous days after Heydrich's assassination, when anybody in Gestapo custody could be shot. However, her father-in-law managed to talk them out of it, but his Viennese partner was not saved—he died in a concentration camp.

After the liberation, Mr. Smolik continued to work for the French and Swiss ambassadors in Prague as a consultant in matters of law. For his services to the French Insitute and for saving their property in Prague he received the Légion d'Honneur, signed by Gen. Charles de Gaulle, the president, himself. The whole family went to the awards ceremony and reception at the French embassy (Ruth included this time), men in dinner jackets, ladies dressed up, and Marie "in full armour," glittering with real diamonds.

"Even the mice down at the old embassy building held their breath, and all the cockroaches in the kitchen wore tuxedos," reported Jan later.

At the time of the champagne toast to *le maître,* Marie noticed Peter's absence and ordered Ruth to go and look for him. She found him in one of the many rooms, fast asleep on a brocaded sofa under the portrait of Cardinal Richelieu.

Peter's brother, later a judge, and his short, plain, but rich wife, Draga, amused their guests with this story repeatedly.

Ruth remembered the fabulous Catholic wedding they had had and, years later, the Catholic christening of their two children—and no objections on the part of the Smoliks.

Once, on the orders of Magdalena, Jan came to help. Peter was at his colleagues' party alone; Ruth was pregnant again. She was unable to reach him, not knowing the name of the friend at whose home the party was taking place. Ruth was bleeding excessively the whole evening, and her temperature was rising. She 'phoned Magdalena, who arranged fast transport to the hospital and ordered Jan to go immediately and baby-sit until Peter returned, which was in the small hours. Ruth had a stillborn son, and again her husband was not with her.

Ruth found it impossible to talk frankly to Peter about her anxieties and how insecure she felt. He didn't have any such problems himself; he knew next to nothing about psychology, complexes, and such and would not take hers seriously. Gradually they grew apart. It was a slow, painful process.

14

Edward died in June 1946, on Beatrix's forty-ninth birthday. In his desk a present was found, marked "for Beatrix"— her last gift from Edward, who never forgot her birthday. When she lost him, she lost everything. In her eyes he was always her young lieutenant, the best man in the world, and she missed him terribly. After his death she carried a kind of perpetual sadness about her.

The Smoliks did ask her to come visit; she declined. She never forgot how cowardly they had behaved towards Edward, Ruth, and the children. But Ruth had to go on to live amongst the family Smolik for the sake of the children and forget her grievances.

The following winter Ruth was in bad shape and both boys had whooping cough. "Off to the mountains with you all!" was Magdalena's order.

To be at the right altitude for the children, Ruth had to stay with them in the village. Peter went with his friends to a chalet higher up in order to have better skiing terrain and did not care to come down to see them. That was the man whom she had hoped to hold her always. Thus the fifth year of Ruth's marriage went by.

There was a military sanatorium in the village, where the Czech soldiers from both fronts were convalescing. Ruth met some of them in her hotel, whenever they came to have a drink there. Major Zelený had served as a pilot in England, so Ruth used to chat in English with him. He offered to take her little boys for rides on the slides and built snowmen for them, so that she could have a rest; the boys were still bothered with coughs at night.

Ruth thought, with sadness, *This is what Peter should be doing.* Major Zelený kept the boys amused and also took some photos of them with Ruth.

After some weeks back in Prague, Major Zelený 'phoned to apologise for his silly fiancée: "She just saw the photos I took of you and suspected us of having an affair; I told her who you were and that it was absurd, that you are married to a lecturer at the technical college, but she made a jealous scene, went to your husband's office, and told him to curb his wife or something."

"My husband never mentioned to me that he had a visit from your young lady. He also must have thought it ridiculous; that surely should calm her down."

Peter never said a thing about this; was he so sure of Ruth, so indifferent, or sure of himself as the ideal husband? She wondered.

Whilst dusting his desk, Ruth saw Peter's diary open—he was always a very untidy man, still accustomed to the maids back home. Also, by now he had forgotten she could read shorthand; it said: "My wife [not "Ruth," but "my wife"] and the children are in fifth place among my interests."

So that's how it was. Ruth was so upset she was determined never to look in this diary ever again. "It serves me right," she sobbed. Now she remembered what Aunt Bertha had said about Peter and what she used to advise girls: "Just you watch the young man, how he treats his mother. That is how he is going to treat you one day." Peter treated his mother, Marie, with impatience, slight contempt, and sometimes standoffishness—certainly not with love and respect. In fact, she never had done much for him. He hated her snobbery, her love for jewellery, but Ruth was quite different, certainly better-educated. His attitude worried her, because he was a bad example to his sons.

Petrol started to become available, so Peter had two motorcycles, an old sports car, and his father's limousine to toy with—another hobby. He never noticed that Ruth had nothing but the never-ending sacred housework—he would not talk about it; "a conversation for kitchen maids," he called it. Ruth hardly had time to read the newspaper, let alone concentrate on a book in some foreign language. She thought she had no more brains. Food was still rationed, and there were no supermarkets. Shopping, standing in the queues with the children, took up a great deal of her patience. *How on earth would I be able to go to work again?*? she wondered.

Ruth watched her former standard of living slipping away in spite of the war being over. She was expected to accept the lot that had been ordained for her and give up everything she liked or wanted to do. Dear Edward had meant to give her the education of a future socialite—in any case, she missed her calling.

Peter didn't care, nor had he noticed that something should be done for his wife's morale. The Equestrian Club was reopened and he went riding in the mornings, budget or no budget. Ruth waited in vain for him to offer it to her as well; they used to ride together before. After all, she was the one tied up at home, lacking the company of adults. Two afternoons a week Peter gave no lectures.

"Would you stay with your darlings? I would like to go riding, too. As you never offer me time off, I'll take it," Ruth told him.

Peter looked surprised, but Ruth's eyes indicated that she meant it.

Ruth met some new friends and was welcomed by some old ones. She soon regained her wit as well as assurance, from the attention and a few compliments received, which stopped her feeling like a zombie. A surprising comradeship developed between her and Renata, her former, slightly younger colleague, in spite of their different backgrounds and status.

"I'll give you the benefit of my own experience. Indifference and neglect from a husband are just like a beating; they cause depression and misery. I wonder how long it would take to make him a cuckold. Make him jealous; he's asking for it," Renata advised.

"No chance. He is not afraid and knows I would never walk out on the children. Besides, it is independence I seek. What I need is my confidence and self-esteem back—I am not after a lover." That was Ruth's firm answer.

"Are you afraid to be happy because it never lasts? I still would go for it over hill and dale and face the harsh reality later."

"Well, I think I am monogamous by nature," said Ruth. "I had to come out of what was a frightening experience more adult and stronger; I would not risk another one."

Renata became Ruth's confidante and friend, just what she needed. She was good-looking and had the figure of a model, the proud profile of an Egyptian princess, natural auburn hair, and a heart of gold. She was a good listener and had a philosophy of her own. She never looked as if office work or any other work made sense to her. Her firm opinion was that love was just a four-letter word. After eight years of childless marriage, she divorced her decent husband for no reason she could think of—she just didn't want a husband. After that she had many beaux to whom she was mysterious; they thought of her as a "maneater"—which was a slander.

"It's easy; just take yourself out of yourself. Time is our enemy; I don't want to die without ever having lived," Renata proclaimed.

As each year passed without the prospect of a better one coming, Ruth was glad it was over. With a sense of waste, she disliked celebrating it. Besides, since she was not able to entertain, they were not invited to friends' parties anymore—they had hardly any friends left. From time to time Ruth let Peter baby-sit, took her apron off, and went to the English Club to brush up her English and have a change of surroundings.

One evening a member approached her and asked, "Can you take care of a new member, my friend Kristian? At his age, forty-six, he wants to start riding."

Ruth agreed to take him along next time she went riding to introduce him to the trainer.

Kristian Richter was a civil engineer, a well-groomed man, not too tall. His hair was prematurely white and his eyes blue. They lit up when he met Ruth. Now Ruth was a skinny thirty-one-year-old mother of two and very lonely. Finally, she didn't know whether it was she who took care of Kristian or he of her. He started riding and she laughed about the bruises on the inner sides of his knees—every beginner's problem.

They also joined the amateur theatre together (which Peter sneered at); they went to the opera together (which Peter disliked). Kristian partnered her for dancing at the English Club's parties (for which Peter did not care). Peter never wanted to go there in spite of the fact that his English was at least as good as Ruth's, even when a retired aunt was willing to stay with the boys sometimes.

So far Ruth's married life had been spoiled by events

neither she nor Peter could control, but it was Ruth alone who had had to take care of all the necessities. From now on she expected Peter to let them both have some social life and enjoy some sports together while they could, as they used to do before. But Peter had other interests in which Ruth could not join him and kept shaking her off.

That was why Ruth grabbed the little freedom she now gained, and Kristian became her *cavalier-servant.* She had forgotten her repressed childhood, her bad times in wartime, and was ready to look after her personal happiness, because no one else would. She was determined to make up for the lost years.

Ruth's new friend was showering her with attention, giving her small presents and flowers, composing rhymes for her, and speaking French with her—"the language of love," he called it. What woman would not like that? All of a sudden things were easy. Ruth engaged the retired aunt to help three afternoons a week and gave private lessons in French to a group of young girls. She felt free as a lark and was again "quick as a flying squirrel"— her nickname at Air France.

Peter didn't notice how cheerful she had become, just as he had ignored it when she was down. She managed the household and never neglected the children, and everything ran smoothly; if not, that he might have noticed. She went riding with Kristian regularly. Sometimes, on sunny days, he would take her with him to spend the day in the country, where he and his assistant were measuring for a road project. She also helped by holding the pole or preparing the picnic or just sat in a deck chair appreciating the outdoors and reading.

Kristian loved her and she was walking on air. She could not be regarded as a sinner—she was someone who needed a little kindness so badly—and Renata was happy for her, especially when she had an opportunity to meet Kristian occasionally and judge for herself.

Ruth confided to her, "He is not free either; he and his wife have lived apart for quite some time. She refused to stay where his work was and did not follow him to their flat in Prague. She felt more comfortable at her parents' large country house. Kristian was not welcomed there by his father-in-law ever since he married her, but that does not prevent his going to see his three teenage children every other weekend."

In the spring Kristian had to go to Brussels for several weeks as the UNRRA supply of building machinery and equipment and the takeover of the Caterpillar bulldozers were negotiated for Czechoslovakia. Before he returned, Ruth left for a camping holiday with her family and had to stay for the summer in Magdalena's country house with her in-laws. Not even phone calls from Kristian were possible. Ruth missed him dreadfully—what an endless summer that was.

At the very back of the garden was a large walnut tree. Whenever possible, Ruth sat in its shade to read the translation of Daphne Du Maurier's *Frenchman's Creek,* which Kristian had given her with the words: "You are very much the heroine: Madame St. Columb. You are also a keen rider, and pirate or no pirate, you'll always go back to your children." This way she felt in touch with him.

The summer was followed by a golden autumn, and before it became too cold, Beatrix wanted to visit her cousins living in Wroclaw (Breslau), Poland. She asked Ruth to come with her, as she would not dare to travel alone. The people there still lived literally in ruins the best they could. Also, the cousins had a house without a roof, temporarily repaired with boards. The vast devastation of that country was depressing. The Poles were rebuilding as fast as possible, yet not fast enough. The trip back by train was long and tiring, and Beatrix wanted to go straight to Prague by an express train.

At the same time, Kristian was with his staff in Zakopane for four days to instruct the Polish builders who also received the UNRRA building equipment. It was convenient for Ruth to meet him there and help with the translation of instructions on the American film demonstrating the use of the building equipment. "I got myself a small job as interpreter," she informed her mother, who was safely on a direct train to Prague.

Ruth could work perfectly with Kristian; he never shut her out as her husband did. On the contrary, he was glad she was interested in what he was doing and appreciated her capability to help. They had a hard day, and Ruth was still exhausted after her journey.

He had a large, comfortable room in one of the hotels that was still standing. She did notice the very old-fashioned decor the colour of terra-cotta. After coming out of the shower, she fell into bed and was immediately asleep in Kristian's arms.

He joked about it gently in the morning.

"After seven years of marriage and two children, you are virtually a virgin—it's unbelievable; you just slept like a baby."

There was no hurry. Ruth *did* eventually find out that she was not frigid, as she had always thought; she just had to be handled especially gently and in the right way. It was important for her to feel "normal" and alive.

"To be with you is to live, to exist, to experience quite new feelings," Kristian said.

While outside it was late autumn, this was the summer of Ruth's life—her best year.

A very cold winter came earlier than usual. Ruth and

Kristian both were back at their duties, and they could meet only occasionally, when the day-to-day work allowed.

One frosty night after their visit to a play rehearsal, Kristian walked Ruth home across the bridge by the light of the full moon. The floes on the river moved with the current. The couple walked through the park and sat on a bench, their boots covered in snow. Their quiet conversation was abruptly interrupted when the bells of Saint Vitus Cathedral chimed 3:00 A.M.

"Kristian, we are demoralising the bats; let's go home," Ruth said. She could not understand how it was possible they didn't feel the cold, nor could she say what they were actually talking about for so long.

They hurried to Ruth's house. She entered stealthily; all were silent and sound asleep. If Peter was not, he pretended to be. He didn't want to know. He would not discuss anything disagreeable; he didn't care for an explanation—it was easier this way. His indifference used to hurt Ruth; now she had become immune.

Sleep eluded her. She was surprised how little remorse she felt in her heart and was dreaming about the impossible—having Kristian for her husband. Only that would make five unhappy children, as she had been once.

Ruth remembered a verse from *Song of Hiawatha,* which she had learned years ago at boarding school in Kingston on Thames when acting in the play.

Onaway, awake, beloved,
Thou the wild-flower of the forest,
Thou the wild-bird of the prairie,
Thou with eyes so soft and fawn-like.

If thou only lookest at me,
I am happy, I am happy,

As the lilies of the prairie,
When they feel the dew upon them.

Her anguish surfacing, Ruth began to weep into her pillow.

15

The circle of the seasons went by swiftly—day by day busy around the children and the household. Another spring in Kristian's company, another summer when he had to take his family for a holiday.

Ruth had to spend the summer alone in the mountains where her sister, Lydia, and her husband had a chalet. Peter took them there by car together with lots of luggage and provisions, came to see them for one weekend, and did not return until they had to be taken back home again in two months' time at the end of August.

In addition to her boys, Ruth had to look after little Lydia, her niece, who was four. The children were happy there running around freely.

"There is a snake on the stump watching us," Simon came to tell Ruth one day. It was a hot day and a viper had come out in the sun.

"Simon, this is a bad snake. Don't play in the tall grass; play ball here, where it is cut. I'll finish the lunch for us, and then we can go to pick some blueberries. In the meantime, you watch Bernard and Lydia," Ruth commanded.

Food was still partly rationed, and Ruth had to take the children with her when shopping down in the village. It was quite a climb back up again. Slowly, up and up with the children and the load in a rucksack, it was a strain.

On one occasion they were caught halfway through

the wood by the storm; the strong wind bent the trees, branches were falling around them, and they were soaked right through in minutes. There was nowhere to hide, and Ruth could not turn back either. Simon was not so frightened, already a reasonable boy. He helped her to calm down the other two, and they walked as fast as possible. Back at home they ended up in bed with hot tea but no temperature. Ruth read them a bedtime story as she did every evening, and they slept all right.

She was uneasy alone in the middle of a wood, not only lonesome, but scared, too, and realised her great responsibility so far from any help. She cooked and washed and was caring for the three demanding youngsters all day long. She swore to herself that she would never do this again—holidays together with her husband—or nothing.

In September 1950 both Ruth's sons went to school. Simon was a clever, alert, lively boy, loved the company of other children, and was happy at school, but Bernard made a scene every morning, crying; it took him longer to adapt. But now was the time for Ruth to gear herself up and return to a full-time job.

The Czech Academy of Sciences offered Ruth a good position, and she was glad to be able to work again with a director who did not mind her being rather rusty.

Ruth had to go through the Communist party vetting to get the job. Had she collaborated? Had she been in the Resistance, in the underground movement? Yes, in the cellar, protecting two babies. Was her husband on the barricades? No, in a labour camp. Does she speak Russian? The trade union functionary did not either; how could he "fraternise"? Did she go to the May Day parade? Was her "political profile" checked by the "street committee"? Did she know contacting people in the West was banned? They were penetrating and undermining socialists' progress. It was ridiculous!

* * *

As soon as Ruth had had children she had turned into a lioness defending her young. On the other hand, Peter never had time for them. It was she who took them swimming, skating, riding, and skiing, all of which Peter did better than she. Since she had started work again, the boys had become latchkey children. They would run away from school to go to the funfair, romp in the streets, and slide on the frozen river unsupervised.

The main problem was the two-month school holiday, when Ruth had only three weeks off. Grandma Beatrix lived with Lydia and was fully occupied with her two children. Grandma Marie spent the summer in one of the spas, again accessible after the war.

Unfortunately, there was no camp for boy scouts under the age of ten. Magdalena came up with an idea; her lady doctor colleague had newly opened and ran a camp for smaller children in southern Bohemia—miles from the capital. Magdalena and Peter took the children there, and according to him, they were fine.

A fortnight later, Ruth's motherly soft heart and instinct would not let her sleep in peace; she urged Peter to travel practically all Saturday there and all Sunday back, just to see for herself how the boys were. This time she overruled his protestations.

Ruth and Peter waited by the school building to see the fifty or so children coming back from the playground to tea and watched the children's sedate walk as the teacher in charge led them in. Ruth's boys were walking in line, each holding the hand of a little girl; approaching, they saw their parents but did not run to greet them. Disciplined, they stayed in the line, went in with the others, and took their coats off in the large hall, where each had his coat hanger marked with a picture. Bernard's was a lion (his zodiac sign, incidentally), Simon's a bear, and one of the little girls' hangers had a picture of a goose. The boys took their shoes off and placed them exactly under the coats tidily, went to the bathroom, where there was a row of small basins, washed their hands, took their places at the long table in the most orderly way, and still did not turn their heads to where their parents were standing; the boys waited hungrily for their tea.

That was too much for Ruth; she had to run out, upset. The sight of her "institutionalised" children reminded her of exactly the same procedure as in the orphanage.

Ruth and Peter had an hour with the boys later. Simon was quite enthusiastic. "We made our own small kites with long tails; mine did not fly very high. Bernard has not tried his; he watched mine with Lucy," he told his parents happily; but Bernard was very quiet until they had to leave; then he asked shyly, "When will you take us home?"

Ruth felt sorry for him and was unable to answer that question.

"Three more weeks before school starts," Peter told him bluntly. Bernard's head just went down slowly; he remained silent, but no tears.

"Don't worry; no one will hurt your cubs," Peter said to Ruth.

All the way back home Ruth was thinking about the strong-headed Bernard who, at age four, had decided to throw a tantrum on the main street in the centre of Prague while they were waiting for a tram, because he wanted to go by taxi. She had had to smack his bottom and drag him into the approaching tram, screaming. How docile he was now.

Ruth had very little free time left, so Kristian phoned her office every day at exactly 1:30 P.M.

"Hearing your voice after lunch is the best dessert I can get." Kristian tried to joke; only by now they were so close, she could tell he was down—he had problems at work.

Because Ruth was so busy, it was necessary to give up amateur theatre and Kristian did not accept a role either; the group lost "the black and white," as they called the two of them.

The communist authorities closed down the English Club. Most of the British-born wives went back to England, and their Czech ex-soldier husbands followed them whichever way they could, often illegally.

Still there was the riding once a week, the only time Ruth and Kristian could be together. One day, from horseback Kristian reached for a shrub to pick a flower for Ruth.

"Here, to say farewell, my darling."

"Why suddenly so serious? Don't be morbid; I want us both to care for each other for a long time yet. Silly, come; I'll race you."

The happiest two years of Ruth's womanhood were to end, slowly but definitely. Ruth understood that Kristian was in a hopeless situation; his last project was finished—he had to move on to another. The times were hard for him, as there was no chance of an opportunity in management because since the communist takeover the fine jobs had been reserved for the communists only, whether qualified or not, and Kristian was not a member of the KSČ,* not even a "Radish."

---

*Czechoslovakian Communist party.

At long last, Kristian was commissioned to a project on the outskirts of a provincial town. It became more practical to live with his family again. His father-in-law had died, his son was now at medical school, his first daughter married at seventeen, and the younger one was still at the lycée.

* * *

For a short time, before they were also abolished, the boys joined the Catholic Boy Scouts. Their duty was to go to the Sunday mass and serve as altar boys. Afterwards they would be taken for an outing in the country. Grandpa Smolik had some doubts about it, so they all went to see the boys "at work." They took it rather seriously, except that their rubber shoes were showing under their robes and they fought for the bell, amusing the congregation. The elderly priest took it calmly, turning to stroke their heads and proceeding with the prayer. Grandpa went to talk to him after the mass and found out that they had attended the same grammar school. While he went on to study law, the priest went to a seminary for theology. Grandpa said to him that his family, the boys included, were protestant and was told: "Let the children come to me . . ."

A few years later the boys had their confirmation in the same Protestant church where Ruth and Peter were married. Ruth could not believe how they had grown. She was proud of them and also a little tearful; she was so busy she hadn't noticed the time passing by.

* * *

Kristian's fevered friendship lasted for a time. They exchanged letters mailed via Poste Restante. He wrote poetically at first and with nostalgia. Gradually the poetry turned to prose as their daily life broke through the romance, which was dying a slow, tender death until it turned to ashes.

Never again did Ruth have a *cavalier-servant.* She soon gave up the idea. Those offering their services all wanted her to serve them and granted her little in return. Besides, Ruth had to be practical. Her job was time-consuming, and her sons needed her more and more. All her energy left after work had to be channelled into their needs. Many months passed in the daily routine, and there was no news from Kristian.

Renata explained it all: "No remorse needed—you are not an albatross who never changes partners—now let go. Just remember how the romance started, but be prepared for the end. That is what I do."

Ruth hardly noticed how years passed; she had to think about her daily, ordinary problems and had virtually no time for herself. One morning she entered her office and there were flowers, cards, boxes of chocolates, even perfume, her desk full. She was touched, because she herself hadn't remembered it was her fortieth birthday. She was not a young woman anymore, only a tired one.

Ruth brought all the flowers and gifts home, where there was nothing for her. It was amazing how regularly everybody in her family forgot her birthday, even her mother. There was no longer a card from Kristian. That was not surprising, just sad.

16

An opportunity had arisen to spend the Xmas holiday at a chalet belonging to Peter's college. For Ruth it meant a great deal—no shopping, no long hours in the kitchen, and everybody happy, especially her teenage boys. They were growing up fast; she watched them with pride and laughed when they raced for a second helping at mealtime.

Before New Year's Day it was snowing all morning, but the boys did not mind and went with others to the "nursery slope" not very far from the chalet.

"Would you get the boys, Peter? Please, they've forgotten it's lunchtime. They serve it here only up to half past one, and it is nearly one o'clock now. Simon has a watch, but it doesn't chime."

Peter didn't even try to spare Ruth the worry and went on with his reading; he did not feel like putting on his skis and going as far as the slopes. Ruth had to go and look for them herself. Arriving at the top, she could see the boys down the hill, but they could not hear her calling. She went down, stumbling, her skis crossed, and she fell. The skis stayed on as she rolled downwards. She called out. Skiers came to her rescue, taking off her skis, and one shoe was pointing backwards. The leg was fractured. A stretcher was sent for. Someone gave her a sip of rum. When the frightened boys reached her, Ruth only just managed to ask them to hurry to the chalet and fetch Dad.

But before Peter came, the Mountain Rescue Service slid Ruth down to the village and the ambulance was off with her to the nearest hospital. There she had to stay for six weeks hanging in traction; after that, plaster and crutches. Peter came to see her once, just to upset her by his casual attitude.

Simon was tough, he did not miss Ruth much, but Bernard kept writing her letters with funny pictures, like of coins on a plate, meaning the boys were given pocket money to fend for themselves. He drew an alarm clock ringing at seven o'clock, meaning they had to make their own breakfast before leaving for school; he wrote what they had for lunch at school. His grim humour was upsetting Ruth; she was worried.

Typical of Peter, his maxim was "to do nothing means to spoil nothing," and so the boys often went to see Grandma Beatrix in search of food. They visited Marie just to see what her maid was doing in the kitchen or would buy themselves hot dogs at a street corner.

Finally an ambulance took Ruth to the station. Her leg was plastered right up. She was put on the train for Prague. She had crutches and a suitcase, but no one was waiting for her on the platform. People left the train; she could not get down the steps or carry her suitcase and get out of the station up the stairs, to where the taxis were standing. A railwayman helped her.

"Oh, good, you took a taxi," Peter said, as if Ruth had flown in. The three of them were sitting and waiting for her at home, no food in the house and a mess everywhere.

"Thank you for the welcome home. Simon, will you please go and get some 'take-away'? I am hungry and tired after the journey. Thank you."

At least the boys looked perplexed and ashamed. They had no idea that Ruth had such a heavy cast and could hardly walk; also, they were disappointed she couldn't cook something nice right away.

Ruth would wear a cast for the next five months, so she had to get organised. It was expected; after all, the boys were *her* responsibility.

More disillusion came when the plaster was finally off and Ruth could not stand on her extremely thin and atrophied leg. Magdalena got her a bed at the best rehabilitation centre in the land, and so she was off again for four weeks to the spa in Karlsbad, paid for by the insurance. Reluctantly she left the boys in Peter's "care," but she gave them some instructions this time.

Ruth's long absence from the office worried her—after all, everybody is replaceable—but her old boss did care; he sent her a translation to do so that her brain would not get too lazy and a humorous get-well card signed by all her colleagues. This really helped her to relax. She hurried to write: "Thank you all; I'll be back soon."

Peter never phoned or wrote to her because, as he put it, she was in good hands. Ruth recuperated in that marvellous institution enough to be able to walk only with a stick. After such a circular fracture, that was success. But more miraculously, she was fit emotionally, which had always been her personal problem.

The walking stick stayed with Ruth for the rest of the year. More serious problems were ahead now. The persecution of the "bourgeois" families was extended to her sons because of their background. There were no private schools anymore, and the state schools for secondary education had orders to accept preferably pupils from the working-class families; the rest could do manual and factory work. The communist regime was adamant about that.

It was time for Simon's secondary education (at age

fourteen to eighteen), with no chance of finding a good school in Prague. Peter had friends or former colleagues everywhere; even former pupils of his were teaching there. He could have contacted them but did nothing for his son's sake. "It is unethical," he said.

Not for Ruth; she knocked on all the relevant doors to find a school. She only found a place in one away from home. Simon took it in a sporting spirit; he was an average student but worked hard.

Peter never had the patience to teach his own children; Ruth thought of Carl, who was such a brilliant scholar. But he was far away and could not help her now.

Simon did quite well at school, but Ruth was not happy about it. The school did not have much of a standard, and for the second year Ruth did find one nearer home, so that he was able to travel to it daily by bus.

More worries for Ruth. Bernard came down with influenza. Ruth left him in the morning with a thermos flask full of tea, some cake and biscuits, and a book, telling him to stay in bed, keep warm, and take aspirins.

When she came back at five o'clock, Ruth found him delirious, the book on the floor, and vomit all over. She called the ambulance and held him all the way to the hospital, as he was really ill. It was infectious cerebral meningitis.

Again, Peter was not there when needed. He never noticed the mess left behind or his son missing, just wondered why the dinner was not ready when the distressed Ruth came back from the hospital.

It took a long time before Bernard fully recovered. He missed a whole term at school; his results were poor anyhow. He was clever enough, just terribly lazy. Of course he failed and was not admitted to any secondary school. Finally he had to go as an apprentice to a factory manufacturing batteries. He learnt nothing there but realised during those three years what a wretched life factory labour was. Among all the factory youngsters he looked like a handsome prince, and he was too much of an individualist and sportsman. At the time he was the champion of the republic on a double Canadian canoe, with the chance of representing his country at the next Olympics. Ruth could not help remembering how he refused to paddle on one of the family outings and preferred to walk on the riverbank; that was when he was about seven years old.

In order not to injure his hands and to be fit for the training, he worked with gloves, which the workshop's foreman frowned upon, calling him a sissy.

The World Canoe Championship of 1958 was held in Prague. Peter was commissioned with interpreting. He was able to speak fluent Italian and was assigned to a group of Italian athletes and their coach. To do this, he was vetted by the communist authorities. At the last moment, the organisers realised there was no interpreter for the gentlemen of the press. That was where Ruth came in with her knowledge of German, French, and English. There was no time for her to be vetted, but there was no harm done. This was sport, no one discussed politics, and everyone enjoyed themselves.

After Bernard's apprenticeship it was very difficult to get him into one of the technical colleges. He needed a recommendation from the shop floor, workshop's foreman, and union. Ruth, dressed in an old coat and headscarf (not to look too "posh"), went to intervene. She talked to the chairman of the Works Committee, but he was adamant: "Why should a lecturer's son study and take the place of a miner's son, who needs it more?" he insisted. And the shop steward agreed with him.

Ruth made a rather tearful scene, the easiest thing for her to do at any time—she was worried and tired. "Bernard missed his chance before, because he was seriously ill," she told them, obviously upset.

To Ruth's joy the union sent the necessary recommendation a week later, all signed and stamped. In the communist regime, stamping had become a national disease. Not that Bernard ever thanked his mother for it; nor did Peter admire her effort. It was fine by them, no comment.

Ruth's household began to lose its shine. Peter lived next to his wife, not with her. He didn't notice how the equipment and nice things she had from home were in need of repair or replacement. The boys were growing fast; their trousers were constantly too short, as if they expected a flood; their appetite was beyond Ruth's means. They needed money for their school excursions, holidays at a youth camp, and various sports gear. Ruth's quite decent earnings were far from adequate; Peter left her to cope with it—she struggled. He was content and did not know why Ruth was not, and there was no more Edward to help her.

Ruth was very disillusioned about her husband. He had such a great intellect and knowledge and was so well read but had absolutely no practical drive or ambition. Ruth could never understand his complacency. Bitterness grew inside her, destroying the remnants of her love for him. He was selfish and uncaring yet gave the impression of being a good husband. Only Renata knew him even better than Ruth herself.

"To stay with Peter is masochism. Even in our generation there must be some women bitchy enough to fight back," Renata used to say. She didn't understand how Ruth could stay with a man who had stopped loving her after some five years of married life and in whom she had lost confidence. It was the ultimate sacrifice for her sons. No personal deprivation would stop her unwavering devotion to them. The tattered remnants of Peter's affection tarnished her life. It resulted in matrimonial difficulties on her side, unnoticed or ignored on his, which made her even sadder. If somebody spoke to her in a kind voice, she wanted to succumb and cry.

Once again Ruth adapted to whatever the situation. She did not feel unhappy at work. There she was happy and if the professor did breathe down her neck sometimes, she knew she was appreciated and paid for her work. There she enjoyed esteem and success. Unfortunately, it was to the detriment of her family; arranging scientific conventions, symposia, colloquia, meetings, and international congresses was a time-consuming job. The aging professor was demanding; her accuracy was down, even to words which should not be there—he used to joke about it.

Sometimes Ruth had to go away for days at a time to take care of foreign participants, conversing in several languages with patience and courtesy and caring for their comfort. The professor liked to watch her: "The way you take the coffee around the conference table, it is amazing, not a hair out of place. My French colleague said to me the other day, 'Your secretary attracts people by some kind of innate nobility she has about her, the way she walks, for example.' I was proud of you."

At work Ruth could forget her hurt feelings and the disillusionment stored in her mind. She learned painfully that Peter was not even thinking it was necessary to show her some affection. His attitude was hard to bear. She was losing her self-esteem, being constantly in need of love since she had been deprived of it in her formative years.

Often the work drained all Ruth's energy, yet money was badly needed in the family. Peter disliked talking about their meagre finances. "Why don't you write poems as Mrs. So and So does? She gets a lot of money for it," he remarked.

"Why don't you? You have more time on your hands. I am not that sprightly. My second shift peeling potatoes, washing your socks, and cleaning the bathroom does not give me much inspiration for writing anything. Your mind is not constantly occupied with problems like how to make a cheap but decent meal every day in half an hour. I certainly have nothing to write poems about. I've had a bad day. Don't make it worse."

"Weeping again? It was just a joke."

"A damn bad one, because I would rather do something less prosaic, take my apron off, go to the opera, ballet, and parties as my friends do, and forget the three of you."

After that ugly outburst Peter began striding about, then tossed a few bank notes on the kitchen table. They slipped onto the floor, where Ruth left them, too offended to pick them up. Such scenes and constant friction embittered her. She caught a glimpse of herself in the mirror, saw her tight lips, her face hardened and severe, and told herself, "I am losing my sense of humour. I'll break things next. This way I shall never get rid of my constant expectation of another blow. I wanted to be a dignified wife. Now look at me! I'll get spikes like a hedgehog soon; I must think of my good upbringing."

Ruth knew she was searching for something that was missing from her life but did not try to analyse it. Her companionship with Renata was a solution. She had seen

Ruth chortling merrily in foreign languages, when she was in her element, and understood her well. They had a tea break together, and Renata listened to Ruth's complaints and noted, "Name one happy marriage. I can't! Your Uncle Albert, for instance, he was the model husband in your family. And what did he do? When his wife Julia died he remarried after six months; he didn't even wait a decent year. And where did this woman spring from? He must have known her before. There is no such thing as an ideal husband, except the one by Oscar Wilde," Renata was chatting on rather nervously and then said, "Kristian is back in town. I had better tell you, because Prague is a town of only just over one million inhabitants and you might bump into him somewhere unprepared."

"That is nice—he'll ring me exactly at one o'clock as he used to."

"I don't think so, Ruth."

"Why not? Or has he his family with him this time?"

"Now you'll be upset; I should have kept my mouth shut. He gave up the apartment. He lives with an insignificant woman, even younger than you. I met her—they were walking arm in arm."

Ruth's heart turned to ice.

"It must be a blow to your shaky ego, but don't you see? It was just an episode for both of you. You never had a hope of keeping him; you just don't want to admit it. You both had to go on with your respective lives eventually."

"It was hard for me to get rid of my dependency on his friendship and his company. I missed him." Ruth's voice trembled.

That night Ruth wept into her pillow. Her longing for Kristian was unbearably pointless, yet the next day at exactly 1:00 P.M. she rang his office. A single thought dominated her mind: *I must talk to him. I must hear his voice. I'll brace myself to talk casually; God, I miss him so.* She dialled the number; Kristian answered, repeating his name twice. Ruth's heart was pounding; she became mute and just held the receiver, tears in her eyes.

"Who is calling? Someone has the wrong number." And he hung up.

This is absurd. I must stop this; it is below my dignity. But she could not help thinking of the good days with Kristian and his support and his precious friendship. When she recovered from yet another failure, she thought how this knight in shining armour rescued her from mishandling and how little she knew how soon it could become rusty.

Renata entered her office asking how she was, but Ruth didn't tell her about the 'phone call.

"You look miserable. Disappointments are nothing to build your life around. I think you'll find a way to leave them behind and plough your own furrow. You made Kristian your anchor to replace Carl and because Peter shakes you off. Do try to do without them all."

17

Pride goes before a fall! The farm had long been made into a kolkhoz. Grandmother Rose came to live in Prague for a few years and died there at the age of seventy-nine.

Barrister Smolik had to pay the "millionaires tax,"* and as if this was not enough, he was condemned to prison for hard currency fraud. There he was to stay for four years.

Most of his remaining property was confiscated as part of the sentence, and he was proclaimed "an enemy of the Socialist Republic." That was the end of his wealth. His sons' careers were ruined. Peter lost his position at the college and Jan, the judge, likewise, not only because of their family's "bourgeois" background, but also for their father's crime. The communists, just like the Nazis, always punished the whole family.

After some months Peter and Jan found jobs elsewhere at a somewhat lower level. They were both largely educated men, so it was not such a problem.

New vetting was ordered for Ruth as well, but her boss saved her by saying resolutely, "We do not employ Mr. Frank Smolik, and his daughter-in-law has nothing to do with his offence."

During her husband's years in prison, Marie soon

---

*Introduced by the communist regime after 1948.

realised she had no friends left. Now she could not entertain dozens of people and there were no more lovely tea parties for ladies, attended by a white-gloved maid. They all forgot Marie. She was lonely, and being financially dependent on handouts from her dictator-like sister-in-law, Magdalena, was hard to bear.

Her sons were not much comfort to Marie, so she turned to Ruth. Now she had esteem and understanding for the only working woman in the family (except Magdalena, the doctor). Ruth was capable of taking care of her three untidy and always hungry men after work but had no time for her mother-in-law, just 'phoned her from the office from time to time to exchange news. Marie now admitted Ruth's efficiency.

One Sunday morning Ruth fainted in the kitchen and toppled over the casserole she was preparing. Only Simon heard the noise; the others didn't come to find out what had happened. As a "pioneer" he had first-aid training and it was he, not the strongest of the three, who carried her onto the settee and summoned the family doctor. The substitute arrived, checked Ruth superficially, left some tranquillisers, and at the door, said to Peter, "She is just hysterical," which Peter readily believed.

The next morning she was rushed to hospital for an immediate gallbladder operation. As she was wheeled out of the operating theatre, barely out of anaesthetic, she got a glimpse of Peter, before her heavy sedative took over. He stood there and this was the first and last time in their married life Ruth saw him concerned for her.

Ruth's boss came personally to wish her a speedy recovery, the dear distracted elderly man, and brought a box full of cream cakes. The nurses had a good laugh about it. It was confiscated and emptied at their tea break.

Bernard was unhappy and visited her often, especially when his pocket money ran out. He was very shy and his hair was no longer mottled gold, but his blue eyes could squeeze and cadge anything out of Ruth without a single word. The altruistic Grandma Beatrix was also very allergic to them.

When Ruth came home from the hospital, there was no one to take care of her. Peter could hardly make a cup of tea. Marie visited her not only to talk; she cooked special food for Ruth and something for the others, which was generally welcomed. She was now courageous and practical, managed with just a "daily," and hoped all would be as it had been before as soon as her husband was out of prison.

The good times never returned. No solicitor can do much work in a communist country where there is no private property or private business. Also, he had no more drive or ambition; he was getting old and being forced to live in modest circumstances didn't bother him. Marie was disappointed and depressed. They lost everything except the contents of their large household, including Marie's jewellery. She could not maintain her former standard and had no chance to rebuild their former position.

Their only help, Magdalena, died suddenly in her surgery. This was the end for such a spoiled woman as Marie. She died of heart failure a year later.

Le maître was left alone in the large residence he clung to stubbornly, in spite of the fact that he could hardly afford to maintain it.

18

Xmas was approaching and each year it was the time Ruth disliked most. She could not explain exactly why she could not enjoy it; perhaps it had to do with her lonely Xmases in the orphanage. When she later lived with Beatrix and Carl in the street near the Old Town Square, in the basement of their house lived a widow, their concierge. She had lost her husband and three children in the influenza epidemic during World War I. A very kind old woman, she sometimes baby-sat for Beatrix, especially after Lydia was born. She was a practising Catholic and often took Ruth with her to the church. At Christmastime, there was a market in Ritířská Street, where they sold all the shining and glittering decorations and also sweets, toys, and candles. They would stroll among the stalls, Ruth sucking on a stick of candy. Then they would visit all the churches in the Old and New Town to look at the little Bethlehems in each one of them, and there were many.

Ruth remembered it and wondered why she was sad at this time of the year; there had been quite a few lovely Christmases.

She stepped out of the tram at Wenceslas Square on her way home from the office to look in some of the shops for gift ideas. It only made her even more depressed when she saw beautiful anoraks that she would have liked to buy for the boys, but they were too expensive.

Near Vodičkova Street she suddenly saw Carl, her darling putative father, whom she had not seen for a long time.

"Dad, what are you doing in Prague? It's lovely to see you. Are you all right?"

"Of course I am all right; it's just so surprising you still call me Dad."

"What else should I call you? Let's talk, here in the coffee shop. Why didn't you tell me you were coming?"

"I am staying with my brother Gregor just for two days. I am here for a checkup by a specialist in diabetes. I am retired now, so I have time on my hands."

Ruth did notice how drained and tired he looked, and his hair was grey.

This was the last time Ruth saw Carl. He died out in the country hospital with only his housekeeper to visit him.

19

Bernard tried his wings on his "bargain" holiday abroad on motorcycle, stopping first at Grandpa Smolik's former clients in Austria. They had a boardinghouse on one of the many smaller lakes. There Bernard was supposed to improve his feeble German and work for his keep, but not for long; he disliked the position of a "poor relative" and left to wander around.

It was raining heavily when Bernard arrived in the evening in Salzburg, and he wondered where he could sleep for free, as he could not sleep under the stars. Sheltering under the arcades, he must have looked in a pretty miserable state, obviously a student on a holiday trip. A man started to talk to him, and from what Bernard gathered, he offered him his place to stay overnight. Bernard was wet and cold and accepted the hospitality.

The moment he entered the fellow's room, inexperienced and with little knowledge about those things, the atmosphere of the place did warn him; he recognised the danger of a homosexual who picked up youngsters. Bernard told him, "I must go down to secure my bike." He rode away as fast as he could for two hours in the rain, nonstop, and ended up exhausted in a straw stack at the edge of a field.

He was still sound asleep in his sleeping bag in the early morning when the farmer poked him with his rake. "Nicht rauchen, bitte," he said. Bernard gesticulated to show he did not smoke and must have looked a sight, because the Austrian farmer grinned and waved his arms, inviting him into his nearby farmhouse. Bernard washed there, and the portly farmer's wife brought him a large bowl of fresh milk and huge chunks of homemade bread with half an inch of butter on it; Bernard had never been so hungry in his life.

The farm was only walking distance from the Italian border. Bernard asked the kind farmer if he might leave his motorcycle in the barn for a few days while he hiked around. First he watched the traffic on the border crossing into Italy; then he found a footpath in the wood to avoid it, because with a Czech passport one needed a visa into every country; he only had an Austrian one. He was lucky they didn't have barbed wire with alarms, as there were on the Czech border everywhere at the time.

Once on the road he managed to hitchhike a ride from a car or two, and in the evening he was in Venice. There he bought himself a plate of spaghetti in a cheap back-street restaurant and slept on the Lido beach. It was nice, soft, and warm on the sand, and he was dead tired. His feet felt so cold in the morning, it woke him; that was because he forgot about the high tide and half of his sleeping bag was soaked already.

Now Bernard wanted to see as much of the famous Venice as possible while he was there, which he did in record time before going back on the road. There he was lucky; he stopped a car going straight back to the Austrian border as he needed. The people stopped to have something to eat. Bernard took one look at the restaurant and asked that he be allowed to wait in the car. It was late afternoon and he had had no lunch, but they understood and invited him to tea, which he accepted, a little embarrassed. Another embarrassment came when he asked to leave before they reached the Austrian border—he only had *one* entry visa.

Bernard sneaked the same way through the wood back into Austria, again grateful there were no wires there as around the Czech border. He picked up his motorcycle and a food parcel from the farmer's wife, who said, "Da hast du; Studenten sind immer hungrig."

"Danke," said Bernard. He was back home in time for his entry examinations at the university.

20

Both boys went to ballroom dancing classes. Bernard was shy with girls; he practically had only one partner, the statuesque Alice. She was nearly as tall as he. At the competitions they looked splendid; they matched as well as a pair of the queen of England's greys.

Alice was nearly finished at the university, while Bernard had only started after the loss of three years at the factory. To his chagrin, she rather coarsely refused to be his girlfriend. After this wound to his pride, he was tough with girls in general.

Simon, on the contrary, was an expert at chatting up the girls. One of his girlfriends, Lucy, a professor's only daughter, asked him about his canoe, and he offered her an outing in it and camping with his party by the river.

After that, she pestered him. She kept 'phoning him, disturbing his studies, and dragged him out of the university library. She guarded him jealously and made scenes in public if he looked at a girl. Simon made fun of it and was flattered, but Ruth sensed danger.

Once on the 'phone she told Lucy, "I am sorry, but my son has a lot of studying to do now. Your father would surely tell you that. Simon will ring you on the weekend." Ruth felt just like her late mother-in-law.

Lucy rang an hour later; Simon did take the call but could not shake her off. She was a spoilt, selfish girl—good-looking, though.

Ruth was no longer her boy's confidante; she knew nothing about Simon's visits to the professor's house each time they went out. She turned to Peter for help, in vain as always.

"The girl is from a good family; you worry too much. They are over eighteen, after all, but let's invite her for an outing with us. I'll talk to her."

Lucy came and didn't even try to hide her boredom. When Peter talked to her about Simon's two more years at the university, she answered with disrespect, "I don't care if he has a degree or not."

Peter ignored that remark, but Ruth could not control her anxiety.

"But *I* do, Lucy. I have to work very hard so that we can afford to keep our sons at the university. Simon's education is important to me and to his future," she told the girl.

Peter whispered, "All that is missing is the lorgnette—I'll get you one."

Shortly afterwards Peter received a 'phone call. The professor and Mrs. Klima wanted to speak to him. They met, and without consulting Ruth, Peter agreed to everything. Lucy was pregnant and wanted a white wedding as soon as possible.

Ruth was desolate. By this time the law allowing abortion had been introduced nearly everywhere, but an abortion was definitely out of the question.

Peter didn't care what was involved. He had just decided to buy a secondhand houseboat and was not going to deny it to himself because of some silly wedding.

"First, Simon can't get married in his corduroys; he has to have a decent suit," Ruth decided.

Grandpa Smolik provided a garnet ring from Marie's collection of jewels as an engagement ring. Ruth had to sell the set of silver she had received from her parents and her fur coat as well.

Just like Edward paying for her wedding, Ruth had to pay for the ring, the bouquets, the cars, and the honeymoon so as not to make Simon look such a poor student next to his bride, on whom her father had lavished a reception at the most luxurious hotel in town. It was not a church wedding; Lucy was not even baptised. Her father was a member of the KSČ (hence his fast career).

The young couple lived upstairs in the professor's house, where his wife ruled supreme, and Simon had to adapt.

Lucy worked as a secretary and Simon had the right to a small grant as a married student, which he had to give her. Ruth sacrificed one-third of her monthly wages for his lunches, tram pass, books, and drawing material as he had no pocket money.

At four months pregnant, Lucy declared she did not want the child. Her parents had to prevent her being hysterical about it, and Simon had to be very patient with her; she was jealous about his every step.

"Marriage is mankind's oldest and most vital institution—but umph!" Simon said, still with humour.

On one exceptional occasion, Peter helped Simon on a drawing of a large engineering scheme for his school project; Ruth typed the first part of his thesis. It was getting late; Simon rang his mother-in-law to say he wouldn't be able to come home in time for dinner. The work finished, Peter gave Simon a lift home. He had never been given a key to the house, so he rang the bell. Lucy opened the window upstairs and started to throw out Simon's clothes. Some of them caught on the tree below. She kept screaming like a shrew, "Go to your parents! Don't come back, you bastard."

Simon just stood there; Peter watched with disgust—he could never stand vulgar language. When Simon's books started to fly down, Peter got out of the car and helped Simon pick them all up and they drove away. There was no effort made by the girl's parents to stop her making such an unnecessary scene.

Lucy loved bravado. She and Simon should never have lived in the same town, let alone been married.

Finally Peter, who never worried about anything, began to wonder if such problems would affect Simon's final examination results, now he had come so far, but he decided not to interfere.

His son proclaimed wistfully, "My wife changes her moods with the weather." Simon kept calm and proved to be right. "To be positive, you must give me freedom, not chains. You married a student; now you wait till the Degree Day," he told Lucy, who kept ringing him, pleading, but he was firmly refusing to let her disrupt his concentration, just promised to come back after the important part of his work had been done. Ruth was surprised to see him act so reasonably. His wife was checking on him in the school's drawing hall, followed him to the library, and made scenes in public, yet Simon did not bat an eyelid. He was not sentimental and, like his father, not very demonstrative, so maybe Lucy wanted him to show more affection. Ruth of all people could understand that. Actually, she now remembered that Peter had never told her he loved her; he had just decided to marry her twenty-five years ago.

21

The time came for Ruth to cope with her menopause and its difficulties. Her sex life was unhappy. While her husband slept immediately after the fast coitus, she was left with her eyes wide open. Usually she cried, because she had to go through with it with her fists tight, her teeth gritted. At the same time, her longing for some gentle tenderness was still there. She was the monogamous type, never intending to go astray—it was only lack of Peter's care and her craving to be loved that led to her short betrayal.

Peter never spoke about Ruth's problems; he just left her alone after she was forty-eight. So be it, her body was her own now, she rather welcomed it after so long.

In the autumn it was their silver wedding anniversary. As they had never celebrated any wedding anniversary before, Ruth thought they should go on a trip together, relax for a change, and see what good it would do for them. Her husband would only agree to a camping holiday. She also gave him the choice of country. "Italy, and as far as Sicily," he said, and left it all to her to get the necessary papers, the Austrian and Italian visas, to queue at the bank for the small ration of foreign currency they were allowed to take, to do the packing and all. Ruth would have preferred Switzerland, where she had friends, but gave in.

The travelling by train was tiresome, and Ruth so disliked the uncomfortable routine at the campsites—the queues for the bathrooms and the bad food—but the weather was beautiful and some camps not too bad. They saw a great deal of the famous places on their way and as many of the well-known views as possible. They did not expect to have another opportunity to come to Italy.

In Florence, Peter 'phoned his colleague. He and Ruth were invited to a fabulous dinner; Ruth's stomach had shrunk so much she could not enjoy it, but they both loved Florence and its picture galleries. They continued by train, then took the boat to Sicily.

Viewing Palermo, they befriended a Swiss couple, who approached them wondering what language they were speaking. The man had bet they were Yugoslavs. They all had a good laugh, and it turned out the Swiss couple was also on a silver anniversary trip. The man lost the bet and paid for the drinks.

Walter and Hilda owned a hotel in Zermatt, of all places, so Ruth had much in common with them and talked to them of the town and Switzerland as a whole.

The next stop was the camp at Taormina. The Swiss couple was due there in two days' time. The two couples planned a rendezvous at Walter and Hilda's hotel. In the meantime, Peter and Ruth settled at the Taormina campsite in their sons' small mountaineering tent.

There Ruth contracted salmonella; her temperature was rising, and she was flat on her back in their tent. The second day even Peter lost his usual calm. On his way to the game warden, whom he wanted to ask the way to the pharmacy, he overheard a young woman calling her children in Czech and stopped to talk to her.

"We have come from Alger; my husband works at the hospital there—"

"A doctor, thank God! And a Czech one!" Peter exclaimed.

To Ruth's surprise, a young man was soon creeping into the low tent on all fours. Ruth thought, *He could not have mistaken our old tent for his.*

"Ah, I am a doctor."

"Did you fall down from the heavens? With the lira we have, we could not afford a doctor here. Thanks."

He calmly examined Ruth, took her temperature, and gave her the correct pills. She felt sleepy.

"Peter, I'll be fine now; the doctor will look in on me again later. You had better go to our rendezvous with Walter and Hilda. Tell them we can't join them for the planned excursion to Etna as we promised."

As if there had not been enough trouble on a holiday, the same night there was such a cloudburst that everybody except the caravan residents was flooded. All they had was soaked; they didn't have a single dry T-shirt left to wear.

Early in the morning the sun was out as if nothing had happened. Peter tied a string between two trees to hang out their clothes and sleeping bags. Ruth rested on a borrowed air mattress with a borrowed blanket. Then the Swiss couple came to see how she was.

"You can't stay here in such a state. Come to the hotel; they are not full," Walter said.

Ruth was embarrassed. She could never get used to their financial insecurity, but Peter told them bluntly, "We do not have enough money for a hotel."

"The hotelier is our friend; we'll fix it, and your meals will be on the house. Let's load your things into our car and go," Walter decided with authority.

From then on it was bliss for the recovering Ruth; for the remaining three days she was comfortable, ate her special diet, and watched Peter stuffing himself with steaks and the incredible Italian ice cream she could not have.

Walter and Hilda were pleasant people and their Mercedes was splendid to travel in. They took Peter and Ruth to see Etna, the volcano, where Peter could show off his knowledge about it; to the Greek amphitheatre, where he excelled as a well-read guide; he was a good conversationalist on international politics and knowledgeable in current events.

Even Ruth, who knew about Peter's ability to remember everything he read, was astonished and proud of him. The men discussed the economy, the ladies their grown-up children—a good company all round.

On parting, Ruth sent a bunch of flowers to the couple's room with a thank-you card, and Hilda gave her a set of baby clothes for the expected grandchild.

When it was time to travel back to Prague, Ruth was sad to leave. She liked to watch Walter being so courteous and kind to his wife of twenty-five years. He put his arm around her shoulders, held her hand, and kissed her cheek; Ruth wondered if Peter also noticed Walter's behaviour. Probably not; he was hurting Ruth by obviously avoiding touching her. She would not have resented that and would have been nice to him, too, but no sex—thus nothing! Ruth observed other older men helping their wives out of the bus, the car, helping to put their coats on, but Peter must have forgotten his manners altogether.

Rome was the last stop. The first thing was to ring a bachelor friend they had there, but no luck this time. He was out of Rome on business. They had to make the tour of Rome quickly, with rumbling stomachs, and then go on to Vienna, which was the only place where the banks were willing to exchange the Czech currency. They at last had a decent meal in Vienna, before boarding the train to Prague, and that was the end of the journey.

At Prague's main railway station, Bernard was waiting for his parents.

"Just leave the luggage and go to the hospital. Grandma Beatrix is in bad shape; they say it's cancer," he said.

They had no time to wash and change and just rushed to the hospital, where they found Beatrix calm and smiling. The doctors had not told her that her illness was terminal and advised Ruth that it was better she not know; all they could do was keep her comfortable.

Peter was never good at giving his wife some support. Whenever there was a crisis, she had to cope alone. He said, "There is nothing much you can do." That was true, but not very comforting.

After the short respite, Ruth was devastated. Usually quite collected at work, this time she could hardly control herself, her tears dripping on the typewriter, but had to go soldiering on—a real trooper, her colleagues used to say. They knew little about her personal life.

It was a beautiful Indian summer that year. Prague's parks were in their best autumn colours, and gossamer flew in the already cold air. Ruth's life had settled into the usual routine when one evening Simon came to tell them all excited.

"You are grandparents. I took Lucy to the maternity unit. They told me not to wait. The first baby takes its time, and they don't like young, nervous fathers pacing up and down their corridors. But as soon as I arrived back home, they 'phoned—we have a little girl. So I went straight back again. She is charming, a beauty already, and has a tiny nose like a button." His eyes shone with happy emotion.

Ruth hadn't expected her lighthearted son to be so enthusiastic. Of course, they were all enchanted.

In June the following year Beatrix was temporarily back home from the hospital to celebrate her seventieth birthday with all her family around her. Simon came to present her proudly with his eight-month-old Charlotte.

"She has brown eyes, the exact colour of my Edward's eyes," Beatrix said. She still remembered him tearfully, because this was also the anniversary of his death. No one denied what she said, but in fact, Simon and Lucy both had brown eyes as well.

"A nice name. The American wife of President Masaryk was named Charlotte. When was the baby baptised?" Beatrix asked.

She didn't notice Simon's embarrassment when somebody interrupted and he didn't answer that question. He could not tell her that in Lucy's family they didn't baptise the children and that he was not able to influence it in any way. He also did not want her to know that no matter how much he wanted to save his marriage for the sake of his beautiful child, his marriage was collapsing.

The spoiled Lucy was soon bored with baby minding and went back to the office. Her energetic Moravian mother was now in charge, whether Simon liked it or not. He was devoted to Charlotte, and she showed preference for him as soon as she could differentiate him from the others. She would scream if her dad did not dress her. She would spit out her food, but not if her dad was feeding her; she took her medicine from him and would sit on his lap quietly while he studied, as long as he would hold her.

Whenever Lucy's parents went away, Ruth took part of her three weeks' holiday and with great pleasure looked after little Charlotte at her home, even if there was no holiday left for Ruth. The little one even managed to charm her Grandpa Peter, who had never wanted girls. She even softened Uncle Bernard's heart, slightly. He let her play with his collection of model cars when she, with a question in her eyes, pointed her little finger at them.

Simon came to pick up his daughter, not complaining, but not too happy either; he was constantly reminded by his in-laws that their house was not his home. He preferred to work at the school library and draughtsmen's room. He was rather down and tired.

"Lucy has a holiday due soon. She wants to go to Capri, not a very modest wish, but the professor intends to offer it to her as a birthday gift—not my half of the expenses, of course. Oh, how they complicate my life."

Ruth expressed her opinion about this: "I think such a romantic tour would do you both good. To be alone together for a time, it might even cure your unhappy marriage. I'll take care of Charlotte, if need be; she likes to be with us. As for the money, recently I did a private translation for an American visiting student; he does not mind paying for it in dollars, so you can have the cash. We are not likely to travel anywhere. Go with your wife and try to patch up your differences, for Charlotte's sake, even if it is rather extravagant."

Ruth was happy with the little girl, who sometimes stayed with her on the weekends. If it was because she had only had boys or perhaps, when she had her children, she was worried about the war, later she was trying to get ready for work again, and she had had other interests and finally a full-time job. Now her position was more stable and she could concentrate on the clever little girl.

Charlotte knew that on Sunday when the tall grandfather clock's hands were in a straight line (six o'clock), she must go back home. She would play and watch it from time to time. When Peter took her home in his old car, she would sit in the back with the inside light on and keep asking when he would be picking her up again.

Simon never thanked Ruth for her help when he returned from that holiday with Lucy. He just said, “I was very patient with her— only she was spending too much on all sorts of silly things. I was glad that some of the meals were included in the package, or else we would have been hungry most of the time. She was irresponsible and didn’t care about our modest quota of hard currency.”

22

A preliminary meeting was organised at Ruth's office to brief the Czech staff and participants on the forthcoming International Congress. Ruth's boss wanted her to acompany him, saying, "You must accompany me to organise the accommodations and smooth down the usual confusion with your 'garden party voice.' "

She was working with the preparatory committee, so it was important to go. It was held in the same provincial town where Dr. Tony Daněk, now a prominent heart specialist, had worked for years. One of the Academy's staff was taken ill, and a lady doctor came to see her. Ruth was given instructions about the tablets and a prescription to buy them. They chatted a little over a cup of coffee, and she plucked up the courage and asked if the lady knew Dr. Daněk.

"Of course, he is a well-known doctor and a notorious man, too," she replied with a gossipy whisper. "His first wife soon found out he was a womaniser. She left him after only one year of marriage. To this day they have to keep the student nurses away from him. He married again some years later and had a son. He lost the boy on a school climbing trip to the High Tatra Mountains. It was a terrible accident. We all were sorry for his wife," etc., etc.

Ruth didn't want to hear any more. She felt a pang in her heart. She had been so young then and could not see the menace behind the mask. Tony's son had died in the very mountains where she had so unfortunately met Tony so many years ago.

* * *

The communist regime was slightly eased during the short time when Alexander Dubček took it over, and travelling was somewhat relaxed. In the spring of 1968 Ruth corresponded with her old friends in England and obtained an invitation for Bernard to stay with a family during his holidays to learn English. He had grown into a handsome, tall young man with an aquiline nose and shy manners and could be good company to the young members of the English family. Ruth made all the necessary travelling arrangements and paid for them, and he was off in June.

Ruth was very busy in the office and could hardly control her sadness and concentrate on her work. Beatrix was slowly dying, and the doctors could not do anything about her condition. If only Ruth had the ability to pray for her. It was just as well that the main preparations for the forthcoming International Congress were finished. Ruth had to do some more hotel reservations, order the flowers for the ladies, and do a few minor other things.

* * *

After long suffering, Beatrix died on August 18, 1968, hoping to be reunited with her dear Edward after twenty-two years; Ruth wished she would be but did not believe in such things. Her mother still looked beautiful on her deathbed, and the distressed Ruth felt as abandoned as when she was left in the orphanage. She sobbed uncontrollably, which Peter could not understand.

"We'll have a waterfall for a week; you are such a bundle of emotions. We all have to die," he said.

Ruth's problem was still the same. Her deprivation syndrome remained for life. Carl had explained it to her when she grew up— what did Peter know?

There was no relief, no end to troubles, just blow after blow. What a terrible year this was. It turned out to be an extra bad one for Ruth and her family, but it was also a fatal one for her native country. Events crashed on them one by one.

At dawn on August 21, 1968, sudden Soviet occupation awoke the capital with aircraft roaring all over the skies. It was shattering to see the tanks under the windows of Ruth's flat again, thundering in the streets of Prague. The radio commentator kept saying, "Keep calm; the president, Gen. Ludvik Svoboda, left for Moscow with General Secretary Alexander Dubček, to negotiate with the Soviets. He warns you against any provocation and wants no bloodshed."

The next day was Beatrix's funeral at the other end of town. There was a general strike as a protest to Soviet occupation, and the whole of Prague was paralysed. Nothing was to move, not even the trams. People stopped the cars in the streets. It was very difficult to get to the crematorium—only eight members of the family arrived in time. They were all stopped several times to explain that the crematorium workers were not striking. The noise from outside was so loud it drowned out the music in the crematorium. It was impossible to say good-bye in peace; the roof nearly came down—such was the noise of the military aircraft day and night—and the sound of the marching army became deafening.

Ruth was promoted shortly before the Academy of Sciences started to organise the International Congress and was involved in the preparations for a whole year. The Congress had only just begun when the Soviet army marched into Czechoslovakia and it had to be cancelled. All the foreign participants* (approximately two thousand) were leaving in a panic, by convoys of cars and coaches, protected by their respective embassies and the Red Cross as far as the southern border leading to Vienna. There Swissair was ready, waiting for them. The trains were not running, all aeroplanes were grounded, the airports were closed for any landing except military, and the bridges over the river Vltava (twelve of them) were guarded by Soviet soldiers, who did not even know exactly where they were.

The Dutch ambassador's residence was on the street where Ruth and her family lived. His children often came to look for their dog, Carton, who loved to run into Ruth's garden. After the fateful morning, Ruth passed the residence on her way to work. The ambassador himself was helping the driver to load the limousine. She stopped, tears running down her cheeks. "Are you leaving us, Your Excellency?" she asked.

"No, I am only sending the children to Holland. How is the Congress going?"

"I am afraid it will have to be cancelled. The committee will decide this morning."

The 'phone in Ruth's office did not stop buzzing; the

---

*The Soviet ones were summoned to their ambassador, Czervonienko.

hotel reservations had to be cancelled, the transport organised, the excursions stopped, the bookings for the ladies' committee and sightseeing cancelled. It was hectic. Ruth had to forget her personal problems. Everything was in a turmoil.

A young American, who obviously had not been in World War II, was so upset and terrified, he dared not leave the hotel when it was time to go. Ruth spoke to him in her air hostess manner, which she had used for frightened passengers. He was finally on his way to London and thankful to Ruth; he took a letter for her son to be posted there. "I'll leave it open, in case of some controls. I just mentioned that his grandmother died, and he should not return at the end of August as planned, but wait until we contact him again," Ruth said.

"Your son is lucky not to be here. He is safe in London. I have received most of my money back now—I'll slip a cheque for him in the letter before I mail it. Thank you very much and good luck!"

His forehead still sweating, the American was off to safety.

It was not all without bloodshed. There was student unrest; boys jumped on top of the tanks; there were clashes as they were waving the Czech flags. It resulted in the young Jan Palach setting fire to himself in Wenceslas Square as a protest. While the Czech army was locked in the barracks on president's orders, people witnessed the treatment the Soviet soldiers received. One was run over by their own tank by accident—the officer shot him on the spot, as if he were a dog. Some fell from the bridge into the river—if they had not been helped by the Czechs they would just have drowned. What an army that was.

23

At long last it was Simon's Degree Day in Prague. Ruth was very proud of him; only, watching the professors' procession passing, she regretted that her husband, who could have been amongst them, was not. It did not bother him in the least; he never was ambitious—but he did appreciate Simon's B.Sc. after all the obstacles his son had had to face.

The widowed Grandpa Smolik hosted the celebration, which, unfortunately, was spoilt by Lucy's bad manners. She chose the restaurant, the meal, and the wine as if she had all the rights. Because no one stopped her, Ruth said nothing either; it would have spoilt the evening even more. Further disruption followed when immediately after the meal Lucy decided to go to the cinema and dragged Simon with her, leaving the family group rather astonished with the unfinished bottles of wine she had ordered. To Ruth's surprise, Grandpa Smolik, whose treat it was, did not object.

Ruth only wondered what her mother-in-law would have said on Peter's Degree Day if Ruth had behaved like that. At the time Ruth did not even dare to ask if her parents could be invited to the celebration.

Times had not changed in Ruth's favour. Now *she* was the "matron" over fifty and a grandmother. Now she should have been respected by her family for her merits—only no one thought of it.

Immediately after his Degree Day, Simon left for his postgraduate training at an atomic power station in England. To enable both boys to study in a foreign country, Ruth had had to get written approval for them from the Ministry of Education. They would issue it only with the consent of the Ministry of Defence, saying they would postpone the boys' compulsory military service for a year. This was a struggle, but Ruth obtained the approval, together with the prolongation of their visas, so that they would be in England legally. This represented quite a task in a communist-run country. They continuously strangled people with red tape.

The following spring Lucy visited Simon in England for ten days. After she had spent his monthly grant, she said she didn't like England. They arranged to spend a fortnight at the end of the summer at a pleasant sea resort in Yugoslavia, where she would come with little Charlotte.

Lucy's next action was to begin secretly seeing her old flame, and she sent her parents with Charlotte to Yugoslavia instead. Simon didn't like it but travelled all the way from England to see his daughter and ignored the hostile attitude of his in-laws. He was by now used to all kinds of eccentric behaviour from Lucy and did not suspect anything serious, just another whim of hers, he thought. It didn't spoil his stay with the charming child; they had a glorious time on the warm, sandy beach.

Disasters tend to come in threes. There was no respite.

It happened during one of the weekends Charlotte came to spend with Ruth and Peter. She used to rush in and ask what surprise they had for her, as there had to be one each time.

"I made a new pink dress for you; we'll go to the special

children's hairdresser to cut and blow-dry your fringe; then we'll go to a puppet show," Ruth said.

Peter thought Charlotte looked so pretty, he took a photo of her and one with Ruth, too, not suspecting it was their last one together. As usual, Charlotte was unwillingly leaving her box of toys that she stored at her grandma's and wanted Ruth to come home with her to show off her new dress. As they arrived and got out of the car, they heard some argument in the house.

"What's the fuss?" Peter wondered.

Lucy opened the door and shouted, "Your wretched son rang up! Ha, ha, ha! The bastard remembered our wedding anniversary! I'll divorce him, the son of that Jewish witch!" She pointed at Ruth.

Lucy pulled the shocked, screaming child into the house and banged the door, leaving the two older people outside stiff with surprise; they could hear poor Charlotte still crying and mumbling something about her new dress. Ruth ignored the insult, but the mere word *divorce* made her whole body shrivel up; it gave her goose pimples.

"That wench is crazy! I'll ring up the professor and warn him; I'll have the child removed from her and remind him we have lawyers in the family to do it. If she wants a divorce she can have it!" Peter was very angry but realised he couldn't interfere—all this was his son's business.

Still awestruck, Simon rang Peter in the evening, also extremely upset: "Please, Father, take Charlotte away from Lucy's furious scenes."

"I can't do a thing; it must be dealt with by you. Grandparents have no legal right to take their grandchildren, not even temporarily," Peter explained.

"She called me names on the international 'phone, and I don't know why! You know I can't interrupt my postgraduate studies just because I have a hysterical wife.

Besides, I have no money for the journey at the moment. Lucy wants to sue for divorce on the grounds that I have left her, which is ridiculous! Other husbands are on long research or business trips. Will you please get a solicitor for me? I'll authorise him to represent me, okay? This is an expensive 'phone call. Thanks. Bye, Dad."

The sleepless Ruth loved that unfortunate child with painful tenderness and assured herself this was just another outburst of bad temper. Why should Lucy take such drastic measures? There was still hope.

No chance—the divorce really started rolling. It was Ruth, not Peter, who went to see the recommended solicitor to hand him Simon's full written authorisation and instructions.

Ruth was sitting in his waiting room for quite a while. It had a view of the square with the town hall where Simon and Lucy's wedding had taken place, and she remembered how the flamboyant Lucy had wanted the cars to go right through the town centre, not straight to the reception.

Ruth tried to understand their problem: the girl was far too outspoken; she did not have such a cloistered upbringing as Ruth had had. Why this attitude when she had had exactly what she wanted? Simon, a first-class wedding, a beautiful child—Lucy was spoilt, yes, but also intelligent and fairly well educated; why was she so bitter? She should be proud of Simon; his career was promising. Why not let him pursue it? Why was she so impatient? He was, after all, only twenty-four. She should give him a chance. He also needed time to develop from the boy she had married into a man. Yes, he had made a mistake, but he had behaved responsibly—or was this only his loving mother's view?

Ruth's sad thoughts were interrupted and she tore her

eyes away from the park in the square: "You can come in, Mrs. Smolik—Dr. Novák is now free," said the secretary.

The brothers didn't see each other much. Simon was now preparing his M.Sc. in Manchester.

Bernard said in his letters: "My big brother is a workaholic, no nonsense; he seldom comes to see me in London and still talks shop . . . , so why does Lucy not trust him?"

Ruth could not stop the feeling of horror that divorces still provoked in her. She was too emotional about them, perhaps since she had lost her dear Carl due to one, witnessed her little niece hanging on her father's neck sobbing after her sister, Lydia, divorced her first husband, the dentist. Thank God, Charlotte was too small to understand.

Soon Ruth had all the answers. Simon's solicitor easily and soon found out there was another man involved; he could prove it and would act on it. He was forthright in court and said Lucy couldn't put the blame on her husband's temporary absence, because she was unfaithful to him and wanted a divorce for that reason only.

"Lucy went berserk in front of the court," he reported. "She abused me with vulgar language; she showed herself in a bad light, had to be restrained and warned by the judge; she then turned to her own solicitor, who only shrugged his shoulders—she had not told him the truth."

Again, Lucy had what she wanted: the divorce, the custody of Charlotte, child support for her, and a new husband. She remarried six months later and moved out, leaving Charlotte with her parents, who had strict instructions: "No one from the Smolik family is going to see the child again," and Lucy went to live with her new husband, ten years her senior, in a flat her doting father bought for her.

Peter was sad that the grandparents could not have the right to visit their grandchild. She would never visit them again. Ruth cried her eyes out. A few times, they went to a place where they could observe Charlotte playing in the garden, but they had to stop going there. It was too painful for them both.

Ruth's emotional attachments were always thwarted. Now her little granddaughter was lost to her.

24

The country was doomed once again. Ruth had lost her mother, she could not see her granddaughter, and her sons could not return home. Being drafted for two years into the army under Soviet command would be no fun—and they would lose out on their studies. Her own career could be ruined at any time—she did not think she could stand more trouble than she had had to endure already.

It was necessary to mobilise a few friends in England to secure the boys there. Simon obtained an industrial grant and worked at his M.Sc. in Manchester. Ruth could not give him any news about Charlotte, just that she was taking care of the child support for the time being and therefore he had the right to be informed regularly about his daughter. This was done in a very strict manner by his ex-father-in-law, and he did send a photo of her from time to time.

Simon wrote: "I bought a doll for Charlotte's birthday, but when they wrapped it for me I had to run out of the shop—the idea that I might not see her for a long time was unbearable." He could not risk coming back to Prague; the authorities would not let him out again.

For Bernard it was more difficult, as he had no degree yet, but he was lucky. A grant from the Czech refugee funds was available, and Ruth managed by correspondence to get him a place at the Imperial College in London, only for one year, but that was better than nothing.

There was an arrangement between Ruth and her sons. As long as Ruth's letters ended with "zdravstvuyte riebyata," a Russian greeting, the boys should not come back. Their stay was still official, so far, and that was very important.

To wrestle with communist authorities was something of an ordeal. For months Ruth applied again and again for exit visas and other formalities. Five times she was refused—it was all in vain. The communist bureaucrat at the Czech Home Office kept saying, "Why visit your sons in England? Have them come back."

At Ruth's sixth attempt, the stubborn official was not present, just his substitute. He stamped all the necessary papers and asked no questions. The hours of queueing were over, her persistence rewarded. Life is full of surprises, mostly bad ones, but this was a good one for a change.

Ruth rushed to the British embassy and received the visas. Now she had her husband's kind agreement to follow the boys to London until the situation cleared up. He sighed, "It's God's will." Ruth thought it was more her perseverance and her feet in the queues everywhere. They had to leave quickly. It was known that the authorities changed their minds and stopped people on the border and at the airports. Therefore everything had to be left behind, with no good-byes to anybody.

Ruth did not look back as they left their home; Peter looked sadly at his old car standing there. They wrote to relatives and friends from London, later.

They arrived with two suitcases and $200, stayed with very kind friends for a few days, and then rented two furnished rooms. Eight days later Ruth found work in a typing pool. For about a week she had trouble handling the new electric IBM she had never seen in her life before and spoiled many letterheads. She would hide them or fill all the other wastepaper baskets with them. Her own would have overflowed. Her wages went straight towards the rent.

It took Peter three weeks to get a job at a petrol station. Now they had the work permits and temporary residence in Great Britain secured, but they had closed certain doors. They had to be very frugal, which was easy—Ruth was used to that.

In Prague a friend was taking care of the child support for Charlotte from the small deposit left behind, and he sold the two cars, the houseboat, the bicycles, the typewriter, the Persian rugs, and whatever, until Simon was able to send the monthly payments. Ruth started a more detailed correspondence with Lucy's father, who ceased to be so hostile now that he assumed they were not coming back.

Simon wrote from Manchester: "I am coming home for the weekend, hitchhiking." Ruth bought a folding bed for him with her first earnings, so that he would not have to bivouac on the floor in his sleeping bag. She made a Czech meal and apple strudel. No matter how hard up they all were, she was delighted to be with her boys. They were safe now!

Not even Renata, who was a close friend from long ago, could understand. She said in her letter:

> . . . Your flat is now sealed; it will be confiscated, the contents included . . . You are losing your life insurance, your pension [at fifty-seven and sixty , respectively]. You must be crazy to make such a sacrifice for your family; they are an ungrateful lot. One day they will not hand you a glass of water, and you know it! You have always been so selfless. Don't expect any togetherness in your family; there never was any. You'll be isolated. . . .

There was a newspaper clipping enclosed with her letter:

> The Czechoslovak Association of Civil Engineers announces, with regret, the death of their member Kristian Richter, M.Sc. (Eng.).

No one had informed Kristian about Ruth's new home in England. They had had only a few mutual friends; it was all so long ago, Ruth was not even sad for him. She no longer knew how it felt to be really happy, personally happy—this was no time to look back; it was nice while it lasted.

Dear Renata,

I made my decision; it's too late to change it now. Every one of us makes a fatal error in his or her lifetime. I made three. I trusted Tony, I married Peter, and I thought the boys needed me, so I followed them into exile. It is long ago that I expected some gratitude from each one of them; now I don't. I have nothing else to live for but them and I know I shall have to cope with life's adversities alone and I shall—you'll see. . . . You used to tell me don't look back, go forward, be positive, so I did, and you tell me I am crazy, I'll struggle. Yes, I do struggle, but can you remember when I didn't? Ever since I married the wrong man at the wrong time in the wrong country I have struggled—now I have good training for it. So don't worry; just write to me, as since I am barred from visiting my native country, I rely on our lively correspondence.

Love,
R.

25

Finally Peter found a good job in his own field, just in time before despair began to set in. Strangely enough, he was overqualified for many jobs, which in fact was a real hindrance. He was diligent at work, became popular, but hated responsibility, therefore had no chance to be promoted. He was never ambitious or solicitous, such a capable, intelligent, and well-educated man.

Ruth still hoped Peter would do well—she so wanted to be proud of him. He was a great disappointment when, in Prague, she saw him being overtaken by his younger colleagues, even by his own pupils, but once again, he never even tried to adapt and rise. He loved his hobbies and left the day-to-day struggle and worry to his wife—he knew she would cope. The old "agony aunt," Bertha, was right, "the fount of all knowledge," as Edward used to say. Peter never made money.

His work was too far from their rented flat, so they had to move and Ruth had to look for another job nearer the new flat. For some ten months she was exploited by a travel agency, where she had to write letters in the languages she knew (and also those she did not know), typing them in a dark room behind the shop.

From Prague they had bad news. They all had been condemned to prison (in absentia) for not returning to Czechoslovakia when their exit visas expired, and the boys for avoiding their military service. Their way back was closed.

Peter's father, *le maître,* who resented his son's decision to live abroad, died unforgiving at age eighty. His now-neglected residence was taken over by Jan, as there was no such thing as an inheritance going abroad in a communist regime—that was the end of Ruth's millionaire father-in-law. Peter didn't give a damn for his family's heirlooms anyhow, but his brother did.

The first holiday was due to Peter and Ruth, and they were invited by Walter and Hilda to their hotel in Zermatt—on the house—which was really kind. They had a marvellous week there, except that Ruth noticed the other couple's marriage was not so blissful. Walter was drinking heavily and Hilda was ashamed, trying bravely to find excuses for him. He even made Peter, who was not used to drinking, stone drunk.

This time Ruth saw all the places she had visited with Carl a long time ago, but in summer they looked different and much more cheerful. From there they travelled by their secondhand car to the village below the Jura, which Ruth wanted to see so much. They stayed with one of her former schoolmates who had once visited Ruth in Prague and owed her some hospitality.

Everything in the village was modernised beyond recognition. The green was crossed by two asphalt roads; the fountain was still there, merely as a decoration. The women in the village used their washing machines now. The tidy heaps of wood in front of each house were missing. The well-kept houses had central heating and bathrooms and Ruth's former friends were driving Alfa Romeos and Mercedeses; they had colour television sets in their smart rooms, and gardens equipped with expensive garden furniture.

Ruth walked alone by Tall William's vineyards, orchards, and fields, which she knew so well. A campsite was there on one of his fields, now owned by his only granddaughter, and the house had been sold to strangers.

Ruth picked a large bunch of red poppies. It was easy to find the graves of Tall William and his Hortense in the tiny churchyard. According to the dates engraved on the simple headstone, they had died within a week of each other—just as in the story about Philemon and Baucis that Ruth remembered from her school days.

Ruth stood there whispering sadly that she would always be grateful to them and their lovely country for having put some sunshine into her troubled childhood. Tearfully she said good-bye.

"This is not my paradise anymore, and I do not think I shall come back here again. Good-bye, Tall William. Good-bye, sweet Hortense."

The way back was via Geneva. Ruth wanted Peter to meet Camille de Roche–Berger. Her parents were also dead now. She had lost her young fiancé, who died of leukaemia, and only at the age of forty did she marry a twenty-five-year-old ex-boxer. He was extremely kind, a charming man with a hilarious sense of humour, and a good host. He respected and loved Camille and did not mind the childless marriage. They were an incredible couple. Ruth and Camille talked about the old days in England, but they did not giggle anymore as they used to.

Travelling from Dover to London, Ruth looked around at the familiar, calm scenery—this was England—and had a blissful feeling of coming home. She was full to the brim with good intentions and spirited; everybody thought of her as a fighter, so her family leaned on her. Fearing that they would be torn apart, Ruth worked hard until the boys were self-reliant.

She took another job, eight hours a day, pounding on a typewriter, during her lunch break if necessary, the supervisor and colleagues breathing down her neck. After four o'clock she was so exhausted, she would have a little cry in the ladies' room. She was disenchanted with her career, as there was lack of opportunity to use her talent in a foreign country, and it was getting her down to have to work out of necessity and cover the constant shortages in the new household. It was all taken for granted of course—that's what mothers are for.

Out of the blue Simon lost his grant just when he was getting his thesis ready. They said: "The project is cancelled." He 'phoned, saying, "Mum, send me a fiver until I find a part-time job. I am not going to give up now."

He drove a taxi nights and weekends—mostly drunken passengers—and struggled on.

Finally, his Degree Day—he had made it in spite of the odds! *It was the happiest day in Ruth's life;* she was so proud of the jolly young man in the square hat and enjoyed the fabulous ceremony. Her son's name was even correctly pronounced when he was given his M.Sc. diploma, and they all went to celebrate in a decent restaurant. Simon was looking forward to never going hungry again, as a job already had been offered to him. The glorious day was not disturbed this time by the new girl in his life, the fine, serious, gentle Vera, an optician.

Soon they had a wedding in a Protestant church; the reception in Ruth's two-room rented flat, for some twenty-eight people, was rather modest. Ruth prepared all the food herself; Bernard was the best man, driver, photographer, and barman. The young couple went to Austria for a short skiing honeymoon. They both worked and lived economically; Vera was a very well organised young woman.

To Ruth's delight, little Andrea was born a year later. Simon would have preferred a boy this time, but she was a beautiful baby, captivating everybody. Ruth again spent weekends and holidays looking after the new baby, whenever she was needed, as when she was looking after her first granddaughter. This little one was different, as she didn't get so attached to Ruth.

Andrea was taken to the Protestant church where Simon and Vera were married to be christened, and a family reception for ten was held at the new house, hosted by Ruth.

The same year, Peter managed to obtain a mortgage at long last and bought a small semidetached house in Middlesex. In front of it was a beautiful, large cherry tree, which just had a profusion of pink blossoms, and there was the usual English privet hedge. It had a large garden in the back. To start a new home, Ruth had to deny herself a great deal to be able to equip it with everything from spoons to furniture, all from her own earnings, as Peter had to pay all the bills.

She worked now in shipping—a job quite unknown to her, as she came from a landlocked country. Her boss had a heavy Scottish accent and dictated with a pipe in his mouth, smoking like a volcano, which was something to get used to. He also had most work to do at ten to five in the afternoon. Soon she was respected and paid fairly, so that she could ensure their expenses would be covered.

The garden had to be done from scratch, and Ruth, a town person, didn't know where to start. The previous Irish owner had a potato field in the back, probably expecting another potato famine.

Ruth took it seriously. First she borrowed some books

on beginner's gardening and started with very hard work. Peter, who was raised on a "heap of compost" like a mushroom, would not touch it. His credo was *Laissez agir la nature,* while Ruth thought, *Noblesse oblige* and *In Rome do as the Romans do,* because she was aware of her neighbours watching her and Peter as newcomers. If the garden was left to Peter, the nettles would grow waist-high.

> Those of us in the world who were cut loose from our homes, destined to wander, trying to make new homes, are free in one way, lost and adrift in another.

Ruth must have read this somewhere but could not recollect where. It was true; nostalgia was sometimes overwhelming. She and Peter missed the fragrant woods of pines, spruces, firs, and larches where they used to walk in their young days. Ruth remembered when once they walked in the virgin woods of South Bohemia and she was wearing green corduroys, Peter remarked that they were very appropriate. That was long ago, when he still noticed what she was wearing and liked her company. If ever they did go walking in one of the many parks around London, he would go quickly, his thoughts miles away, and Ruth just followed like his dog.

Sometimes they visited all the famous places in London, pretending they were just tourists, ending up in the Wellington Museum, Peter's interest. They stood for hours at the Mall to see the queen on her way to the Trooping of the Colours, Ruth's great interest.

"You are becoming a royalist!" Peter laughed.

"No, I always was ever since I saw the young Princess Elizabeth in the thirties."

If the will refuses to go back to the roots, the subconscious does not. All refugees have nightmares and so did Ruth's family. They used to compare them at breakfast; some were quite funny. In her dreams Ruth often spent the night in Prague. She saw herself waiting for the tram no. 11, which used to take her home from work. *But the flat has been confiscated; I have nowhere to go. They* (the reds) *won't let me out again. I must get to England; my family is there,* she thought. *There is a barred window; I am in jail; how did I get here? Out, out!* And she would wake up in a sweat. The intervals between nightmares became longer, but they never stopped.

26

Dear Renata,

Where we live I can hear the aeroplanes at night heading for the nearby airport, but their sound is not threatening; it is a different sound, not a frightening one.

I went for an outing to Windsor with Peter and sat for a while by the river Thames. Peter was rather nostalgic about his houseboat, which was moored under the Slapy dam, but realised that he could not afford one here and that the scenery is not the same. But we went for a few days as far as the Lake District. Peter hired an enormous tent, probably meant for the viceroy of India, and had great difficulties in erecting the complicated thing. We were glad to have it, as it was raining nonstop, and we saw only a little of this apparently beautiful countryside.

The English people treat us with caution; they are nice but not kind. Perhaps this will change when we have been here longer.

Now Xmas is approaching and I am afraid with my meagre income it will be rather difficult to get a gift for each one of the boys as usual. Maybe this year I am not going to get the customary apron or wooden spoon, which shows how they view me, and, to top it all every year, a small amount of money in an envelope from Peter. That is what they used to give to the maids in his family. Sometimes I feel like burning it over the candles, but what would the nuns say? I'll spend a long time in the kitchen preparing some goodies, and you'll say I'm a fool, how Peter is unimaginative and how they all lean on me, but you never had responsibility for a family; you wouldn't know. But do write to me soon!

R.

"The fervently awaited naturalisation papers are here!" exclaimed Ruth one morning, sobbing with relief. She had always been fond of England since her young days, and in spite of the fact that it had changed badly since the thirties (due to the war and a kind of Americanisation), she had great esteem for it. Now her family became British citizens; she welcomed it with enthusiasm, showing the new passports around, proud and tearful at the same time. It was so important to her; she never looked back to where she had left her unfortunate native country—her own family came first. They were safe now.

A rather funny incident happened at the solicitor's when Ruth went there to take the oath to the queen. As Ruth was bronzed from working in the garden, he handed her the Koran. She protested. He broke off for a moment, then looked at her documents and asked, "Where do you come from?"

" 'A far-away country of whose people we know nothing,' " she replied, quoting Neville Chamberlain. Czechoslovakia is in Central Europe and was formed in 1918 after the Conference of Versailles. But how could the solicitor know? He was born much later.

Dear Renata,

Good news! We are all British—the loyal subjects of Her Majesty Elizabeth II. My family should now belong to a higher echelon, but we are still treated as refugees and can never be allowed out of that subordinate position. I must admit it embarrasses only me; my men don't give a damn.

I didn't expect a very social life here. We used to be invited to parties at the beginning. I felt I was being shown off like an animal out of a cage. Everybody expected us to tell a story, how we crawled on our hands and knees through the virgin forest of South Bohemia. To have arrived at Heathrow Airport, tearful and with a suitcase each, was not interesting. They thought we must have forgotten how to enjoy ourselves, because we didn't join in the singing and tapping at glasses with a spoon.

When I invited our English friends to dinner, I cooked pheasants the way the gamekeepers' wives do—with herbs. They thought it strange, but my apple strudel was always welcomed.

No one admired us for doing all sorts of odd jobs to have enough to live on. Bernard even drove funeral cars to supplement his small grant, but after he finished his qualification, he found doors closed to him for a long time.

The boys will soon leave their nest. Peter was never as involved with them as I was. I have already had so much taken away from me, I'll feel like a flat battery no one cares to recharge. but as you say, "Let go; you stick to them too much"—so I'll try.

Love,
R.

Simon was offered a tempting contract in Canada and had to leave with his family quite suddenly: "No tears for Andrea, Mum; you can come and visit us on your next holiday. It won't be like Charlotte. There still will be some baby-sitting for this one; don't worry." And off they went for the airport.

Ruth was standing in front of the house, waving. Her eyes were strangely dry. "Andrea will not miss me," she muttered to herself.

* * *

Dear Ruth,

You'll be surprised that I am in Egypt as an assistant

to Dr. Marek. There is an archeological conference here, and they'll do some digging as well. Things have changed since your old boss was killed in a car accident, Dr. Marek is more daring with the communist authorities; still, we are not allowed to communicate and fraternise too much with the locals.

I love it here. There are vast sandy beaches, mostly deserted, with green-blue waters in the transparent sea. Here nothing has changed for two thousand years. The men sit at their doorsteps doing nothing; barefoot children run around; the women are working in the fields. You can see a woman on a donkey, baby in her arms and a dark veil on her head. In Alexandria there is nothing much either, no cabins, no kiosks with food and drink; just the large hotels have private beaches. If this beautiful resort belonged to the Swiss, they would make a gold mine out of it. The sanitation here is so backward—we are all ill.

Renata

* * *

Simon and his family loved it in Canada. He found life there perfect for young people, with lots of opportunities for winter sports, as well as water sports in their hot summers. He wrote: "In such a large country it is easier to assimilate and be accepted because here, as in the USA, everybody is an immigrant, except for the red Indians, while in England all this is still quite a problem. For you to move and adapt again would be too adventurous—even Father must admit that, but do come on a visit."

Ruth and Peter visited their successful son and his family as well as seven more Smoliks who lived in Canada. One cousin offered to put his cottage in the Laurentian Mountains at their disposal. It was in a beautiful, quite isolated spot in the middle of a wood, large enough and comfortable. After a few days, Simon decided he would take his wife and his father for a canoe trip down the Devil's River and left the slightly protesting Ruth with four-year-old Andrea behind "in all this peace and comfort."

Dear Renata,

The story is repeated—I am alone with a child in the middle of nowhere, just as years ago in the Giant Mountains with my own children. I am scared and have distressful, sleepless nights listening to the rustle of the trees and all sorts of strange sounds and noises outside in the pitch darkness. I am worried if something should happen to either of us—there is no 'phone and any help is too far away. They all forgot that I am ageing and more sickness-prone.

Little Andrea is a lively, clever child, bilingual already. She rises early, has her cornflakes with milk and raisins at seven o'clock, and we are off immediately to see the "little" cows in the pasture. It becomes very hot later, when we go back for lunch. The freezer is packed with good food—large steaks, fresh salmon, salami, and cheeses—only I have not much of an appetite. I feel uneasy here alone, in spite of all the beauty around us.

In the shade, between two huge maple trees, is a hammock where Andrea has her "beauty sleep" after I assure her that all the chipmunks also sleep after lunch.

The hammock was swinging in the light breeze. Sitting in a deck chair, I watched my sleeping granddaughter. She is going to be a beauty, I think.

In the daytime it is very peaceful. I observe all kinds of strange birds on the wing, buzzing of the insects, the strong fragrance of the firs, pitch or resin mixed with the sweet smell of the wildflowers everywhere—it is overwhelming and soothing. I felt so tired I dozed off until Andrea's voice, asking for a lemonade, woke me up.

The night was clear, lit by the moon. I heard heavy steps behind the cottage—I shivered; it would be so easy for a burglar to get in through the bathroom window, which slides up. I covered the sleeping Andrea completely with the sheet so that she would not be noticed if it was an intruder, and I tiptoed to the mansard window to peep under the corner of the curtain, my heart beating alarmingly. It was a large porcupine that made such a noise stamping around the overturned dustbin, feeding on the remains of food. Relieved, I went back to bed, still thinking what I would have done if . . . I wish you could be with me; you are not such a coward. . . .

R.

Peter and the young couple were back after a week, happy and contented. They had had a lovely time camping in the wild country. When Ruth told them about the shock the porcupine gave her, Simon said, "There is a shotgun hanging in the hall, and it's loaded." Lot of good that would be to an old woman who had never seen a gun except on TV!

While on the North American continent, Peter travelled to visit his friends and also an old schoolmate, now a professor in Chicago. For the others it was time to say, "Thank you," to the cousin and his charming wife for their hospitality, hand the cottage over, and in the evening drive back to Montreal.

On the highway they met with a car accident when a drunken driver overlooked a red light, emerging right in front of Simon's car. He stepped on the brakes, frantically trying to stop, but however hard he wanted to, he could not avoid the collision. It was a deafening impact; it all happened in seconds.

Passing drivers stopped and pulled the vomiting Andrea and the rest of them from the squashed car. They brought their blankets to keep them all warm, and someone called the police and ambulance. Simon was bleeding in the back of his head, Vera had hit her chin against the front seat and her lower gums were bleeding, and Ruth's left arm was hanging motionless, obviously broken.

The police got there first. They dragged the drunken driver from his car. He was still so drunk he could not stand up, but he was not injured at all. Then the police talked to some witnesses.

Simon's wrecked car was towed away. He said, "Poor car, I only had it for a few months." What a funny thing to say. It was just a load of tin. There were his injured wife, daughter, and mother, trembling by the road. Ruth just could never understand her men, never.

Finally the ambulance took them to the nearest hospital. Andrea had to stay in the children's ward for shock and observation. Ruth had an operation on her arm, which had been fractured in four places. Vera's and Simon's cuts were treated, and they checked into a nearby hotel to wait for results about little Andrea.

When Simon rang his father in Chicago to tell him about the accident, his answer was: "If there is no one at home in Montreal, I'll stay here with my friends, and also I want to visit someone in New York." He certainly did not rush to see his family, to show his concern, as anybody else would do, if only for moral support.

Again, Peter was not there when he was needed, but his lack of interest did not make Ruth weep anymore. On the contrary, she had a feeling of bliss, being taken care of in a luxurious new hospital, tended to, washed, combed, and fed by nice young nurses; they cared, even if it was only professionally.

Once a day Ruth was wheeled into the children's ward to cheer up her granddaughter, who was actually quite brave, and Ruth read for her the story of Black Beauty, as this was the period of Andrea's life when she loved all animals, especially horses.

Back in Montreal after two weeks, Andrea had to be checked by the family doctor for her bladder, which caused some trouble. Ruth, her arm plastered up to the shoulder, her ribs hurting, had problems getting dressed. Peter went on visiting places and people and spending weekends out in the country regardless, leaving Ruth behind. She wished she could cancel the chartered flight and go home earlier after Simon said, "Don't let Vera wait on you," which was unkind. How often Ruth had waited on them all, Vera included.

Two days before departure, Ruth angrily revolted; she had to put her foot down to be taken, at least, for a tour of Montreal, as it was not likely she would be back in a hurry. Ruth liked the clean, new town, prosperous and safe, when she finally had a chance to see it, and Peter took her to Niagara Falls, as he wanted to visit them anyhow.

Home at long last, Ruth had to manage her household with one arm only, except for the garden. Peter would not have touched it even if Ruth had no arms at all. It was so overgrown, her heart was aching for it. She had to hire a gardener to put it back in shape. She liked the Irish man; he treated her with respect and consideration, as if she was "lady of the manor," was extremely polite, and did exactly as she wished. Only how on earth was she going to keep it so tidy? She couldn't afford to have a gardener permanently.

The struggle with the insurance company for Ruth's compensation took three years of correspondence between one solicitor representing her in Canada and another in England. In the meantime, she had to have a second operation on her arm, which left it slightly crippled.

When the modest amount of money came, Ruth had

some house improvements done, before she realised it was not appreciated and she was wasting it.

Renata wrote:

> . . . when will you stop this selflessness? You are all you have; give yourself a treat, as no one else will. Don't spend a single penny on the house. The compensation is to improve your damaged health; it is you who suffered for it—you deserve it. It is a good idea to go to a spa; to be alone for a time is going to do you good. . . .

As it was impossible to go to any famous Czech spa, Ruth went for a cure to Badgastein in Austria and wrote to Renata from there:

> Dear Renata,
>
> This is a terribly old-fashioned spa. It has been left untouched since Emperor Francis Joseph's days. It can't be compared with Karlsbad or Marienbad. They don't have any modern medical equipment, nor do they use the latest healing methods. It is set in a most beautiful mountainous countryside, it is very peaceful, and the bubbly bathwater does good to my nerves. Also, I try to deal with my troubled mind. I think about my failure in the relationship with Peter. Where did I go wrong, and why was the marriage left to go, to become a sham, in spite of all the goodwill I poured into it? I clung to Peter too much; now slowly and painfully I "unstuck" myself just to stick to my sons. You said I am buying their love but I can't help loving them; I can't stop caring for them.
>
> My looks fade away; my face is etched with wrinkles. I can form a smile only with great effort. I hide myself behind glasses. There is no place for me in Peter's life—his indifference is humiliating.
>
> Do you think that if there is no longer any physical attraction between couples, if they can't communicate in bed, they can't communicate at all? Does every marriage

become so colourless and mediocre? Must it become such an emotional desert? . . .

R.

Dear Ruth,

I have your letter from Badgastein. I don't think you should have spoiled your stay there with reminiscences; it is too late anyhow. If a marriage goes to the dogs, you can never blame only one of the partners. Your tired spirit, which had to endure Peter's endless recklessness and insensitive behaviour, cannot take any more.

I remember you telling me about your wordless love-making and how you never managed to synchronise the time for it and how you looked aghast at me when I told you about foreplay—you had never heard of it.

I think Peter is lucky. A lesser woman would have collapsed under the hard existence he prepared for you—or left him a long time ago. I know you did think of it at one time but told me you could never "divorce" your children. What use to think back? You have nowhere to go, your sons would never understand why you should, so stop torturing yourself . . .

R.

Ruth came back from her cure with new hope and cheerful, only to find her household and garden in a mess and her careless husband unchanged—it was a rude awakening from the bliss in the solitude and peace of the spa.

The following year a holiday was out of the question, but a year later Ruth reminded her forgetful husband of her spoilt holiday in Canada. Peter never thought to compensate her for it. She worked hard and saved for another holiday and was willing to add some of her insurance money to it. She booked and paid for a coach tour across France, Luxembourg, Liechtenstein, Switzerland,

and Austria, leaving the expenses during the travelling to Peter. It was a very interesting trip, and Ruth loved the wooded mountains and vast pine woods that reminded her of her native country. She hadn't realised she still missed the pine woods.

Peter was soon bored with the tour. When everybody went up into the mountains, he went down to the town; when everybody visited a town, he went up into the mountains. Never with the group, never with his wife like all the others. Ruth was ashamed of him when the coach with some forty people had to wait for him. She could not relax, never knowing what he was up to.

Next time she could just as well travel alone. It was sad for her to realise she was better off without him. He deprived her of the pleasure of travelling and was not good company.

From now on, when rejected, Ruth rejected also. She forced herself into selfishness, which was not in her character. It made her dour; she was growing old and refused to be ordered about peremptorily. Whenever she had a chance to take her apron off, she would go on her own into London, that overcrowded desert, have a meal out, and go to her favourite ballet or cinema. She had to simplify herself, from the psychological point of view. Not that she was complaining. All mothers serve their families; some even get rewarded with appreciation. Ruth did not. She asked herself if it was right to ignore the theory of bringing up children. She played it by ear and brought them up with love and care; they were not problem children. To this day they did not smoke or drink; they were intelligent and good sports. But oh, they did take everything for granted. This they inherited from Peter, she admitted to herself.

It was Simon who had changed the most. He did well in Canada and had a fine detached house, two cars, and a cottage by the lake with a small yacht, and Andrea was in a private school. He became reckless, greedy, dared to criticise his parents and their dwelling, and acquired a rather sarcastic sense of humour.

Simon's wife, Vera, who helped a great deal towards their good position, seemed unhappy. Marriage fatigue perhaps? Ruth was sensitive to the atmosphere they created and felt awkward with them. Andrea became a rather spoiled teenager, sweet but no longer a baby.

Renata wrote:

> . . . I just think back how you cared for your sons, often in uncertain, precarious circumstances, supporting them up to the age of twenty-two. I watched your struggle since they were small boys. You gave them the chance to do well; now they show you superiority instead of gratitude. Simon was such a modest young man, but as they say, "The higher the monkey climbs, the better you can see its posterior. . . ."

In the meantime, Bernard had started to work in the computer business and, with his girlfriend of several years, who also worked in the same line, bought a charming small bungalow in Kent, but they did not get married. The sophisticated Irma waited patiently for him to decide to marry her, but he had this dilemma—he wanted to be looked after but remain free and selfish. He prevaricated too long (as did his grandfather, Edward).

The upwardly moving Irma thought it was tacitly understood she could now follow her own lodestar. Actions speak louder than words. She accepted a position in New York, USA, which was offered to her.

The growling bachelor still imagined he could have the girl on remote control and that sex was the panacea to all emptiness. He travelled to New York by Laker as often as he could, but Irma did not derive such vicarious pleasure from his company, and soon she put it succinctly to him that she would rather stay in New York, where her work was not so stultifyingly dull.

Back from one of his visits, Bernard was very upset: "Mum, Irma is not coming back after her contract expires. She is getting married in New York. I have to sell the bungalow. She wants her half of the money back, and all her personal belongings are to be sent over."

There was nothing Ruth could say to him. Any form of love is rare; he had had plenty of it and hadn't even noticed. He certainly did not take the loss of Irma lightly; he regretted his loss, felt guilty and had spells when he hated the whole world. Only guilt can never undo anything.

Bernard's craving for freedom and excitement plus his egoism prevailed. Happily he remained single and free to pursue his infatuation with fast cars and racing and was fastidious about girls. The measure of love is what one is willing to give up for it—he preferred the "primrose path" and was not going to settle down; after Irma, no other woman was up to the task of being his partner.

Renata wrote:

> . . . Bernard has many sterling qualities, but he is the sort of guy if you say, "Hallo, Bernard; how are you?" he is stuck for an answer. All three of your men have as poor a knowledge of women as men in the Stone Age. If he goes to discharge his anger on his racing car, I hope he's not going to kill himself. When the anger is not an asset he can't win—it gets recycled . . .

27

After years of hectic work, Ruth had to retire. She had planned to stay with the company to a few years over sixty, but it was not possible. Once again she was not in charge of her own destiny, and she retired most unwillingly.

Dear Renata,

I have to slow down whether I want to or not. I can't imagine being "grounded" again as a hausfrau—which means a nobody. I'll miss the work, the people, and my own income, of course.

Although age leaves its marks on a woman's appearance, she still has some pride and feelings. Her dreams, which collapsed one by one, tend to come back. Even when it seems her entire personality was killed off, her spirit is still there as before.

When my men are around, they cut me out of their conversation. "Mum, will you make some coffee?"—the word 'please' missing. They make me feel old-fashioned and vexed.

Peter's old friend the professor from Chicago repaid Peter's visit. He kissed my cheek, and I realised no one had done that for ages. They talked about the old days in Prague, and out of the blue he turned to me with a smile and asked, "What have you been doing all these years here in England?"

I blushed; no one ever asked me to talk about myself. I thought he was just being polite. Then Peter cut in: "She worked in some sort of export business," and changed the subject.

I took the teacups to the sanctuary of my kitchen to hide my tears. As usual I felt wronged and rejected. Who wants to hear how I earned the money to equip our new home? I realised how much I was longing for kindness and a little attention. You see, I am incorrigible.

Love,
Ruth.

Retirement is what most people look forward to. It is the time when it is too late to wonder what one could have been if one's potential and talents were developed instead of being smothered in tedious service to the family. Old age is supposed to be lit up by memories; to live on them should be a pleasure. But if they are predominantly painful ones, it is better to forget the past.

Like everyone, Ruth had dreamt about what she would do in all that spare time—what she would read, what concerts and plays she would go to, what excursions she would make, the friends she would visit. It did not take her long to realise the reality—she was again the dependent maidservant, only a slower one. There was not much she could afford with her shrinking income.

She used all her common sense to pull herself together: "I feel insecure because I am not using my brain, and I must be independent," she said, and she went out to look for work, aged sixty plus.

It took her a long time to find the architect's office where the agency sent her for an interview. She climbed three floors in an old building and came into a hall full of drawing boards and young people. She ran down the three floors again, still hearing the collective laughter: "We wanted a girl Friday and they sent us a granny Friday—ha, ha, ha!"

For two days Ruth was afraid to go out; then she plucked up all her courage and went to a travel agency for an interview. She had worked in that field before, so there was a chance. The boss looked at her as if she was a scorpion and said, "I wanted someone behind the counter," meaning a young Brigitte Bardot—never mind if she did not know the difference between Austria and Australia, Budapest and Bucharest.

Ruth endured the same at a shoe shop where there was a vacancy for a shop assistant: "Not at your age, not with your accent," said the manager.

Each attempt to make herself presentable took Ruth longer. "All right, I am older; that does not mean I am stupid—I must try again," she decided.

The next day, still furious, Ruth went for an interview to a large hotel. They offered her a job as a lavatory attendant—that was the last straw.

Peter would only gain by giving her still less household money if she had some income, and would buy himself another car. He couldn't understand why she wanted an occupation if not for the money. His sensitivity was dormant. He never had any emotional problems himself; how could he know about other people's "melodramas"?

Correspondence with Renata kept Ruth's spirit up for many years. In the last letter, Renata had advised her for retirement: "Tell yourself, 'I am all I have,' and spoil yourself sometimes."

There was a long interval when no letters came for some time, but Ruth thought nothing of it; it had happened before when there was nothing worth writing about. Then a letter came from Renata's sister, a retired teacher. It was brief:

. . . Renata had a hysterectomy. Cancer and death followed shortly after. I don't want to go into the distressing details which always precede this kind of death. You were considered her best friend; she thought the world of you. I am sure you'll agree with me that she did not deserve such an end. She never hurt or disappointed anybody . . .

Nothing could assuage Ruth's grief; she had lost her dear "psychoanalyst."

* * *

Peter retired with pleasure. Beaming with health, he had a huge appetite, was content in the comfort Ruth provided, and had not a single worry. He spent all his time with his hobbies and was not concerned whatsoever that his and Ruth's old age was not secure. That was exactly like his father, *le maître,* and like him, Peter was incorrigibly stubborn in his old age and stopped making his hollow promises.

For years Ruth had had to put up with her three men's assorted bad habits; now she was too tired to rebel. Her seventieth birthday came and went unnoticed as usual, only she didn't care anymore. Just as she used to fight for her happiness, now she fought for peace, which in her twilight years she much deserved. In front of her window the beautiful cherry tree was in full bloom once again, and Ruth wondered how many more times she would be able to see it. The rest of the garden was sadly neglected and overgrown, but peaceful. Ruth was not able to attend to it anymore.

*　*　*

Ruth's native country was free again after Mikhail Gorbachev withdrew the Soviet army from Czechoslovakia. The changes didn't concern her. It was too late. Too many years had passed, and she felt she did not belong there anymore.